OTHER VOICES OTHER SCRIPTS

Other Voices Other Scripts

CompCare Publishers

2415 Annapolis Lane
Minneapolis, Minnesota 55441

Library of Congress Cataloging-in-Publication Data

Williamson, P.
    Other voices other scripts / P. Williamson
        p. cm.
    Includes index.
    ISBN 0-89638-226-5
    1. Sexual addiction—Popular works.
    2. Imaginary conversations.
I. Title.
RC560.S43W55   1990   90-41462
616.85'833—dc20   CIP

Cover design by Jeremy Gale
Interior design by Pamela Arnold

Inquiries, orders and catalog requests
should be addressed to
CompCare Publishers
2415 Annapolis Lane
Minneapolis, Minnesota 55441
Call toll free 800/328-3330
(Minnesota residents 612/559-4800)

  6   5   4   3   2   1
 95   94   93   92   91   90

For S.M.A.

Note to Readers

You will discover many voices in this book—of men and women of varying ages, backgrounds, levels of education, and economic comfort. They are the true voices of ordinary people in Twelve Step recovery, who are working courageously to overcome a problem that has seriously affected their lives.

Each person is involved—as we all are—in an inner dialogue, a "conversation with oneself." The voices printed in italic represent the kinds of scripts we continue to "hear" throughout our lives. Often the voice is the admonishment or scolding of a parent or critic or other authority figure. Sometimes it is the voice of recklessness, or discouragement, or low self-esteem. Or it is simply our "conscience."

For each of us, the voices that sound most often in our thoughts are unique—and an essential part of who we are. The thoughtful inner dialogues in this book become a healing process for the readers. These dialogues can lead us to a deepening awareness of our human complexity and, eventually, to a resolution and harmony within ourselves.

Introduction

Sailors talk of voyages as passages, and we can make the same comparison, here, in this book of explorations. In the readings that follow, we are taking a journey, seeking new adventures and visions of ourselves, expanding our horizons, taking risks, and always trusting we will come safely home. All these moves are passages, and we know they will be arduous, even perilous, but at the same time we trust they will be inspiriting and, at the end, serene.

This is a book of many voices, female and male, adult and childish, painful and angry, joyful and strong. These voices come from many lives and represent many sides and perspectives of a multitude of people. They will be heard especially by those of us who are burdened by addictions and who are or who desire to be in recovery. They speak to anyone seeking to understand more fully what it is to be human.

One particular addiction that invades and dominates the lives of many men and women is addiction to sexual acting out. We can say that we are sex addicts if we feel driven by sexual fantasies and acts that are destructive to our values and to ourselves and others. Sex addiction is not defined by intensity of desire, choice of partner, zone of pleasure, or frequency of sexual performance. It is a demonic force that drives us, insistently and obsessively, to seek a sexual stimulus that holds out, like a talisman, the seductive promise of a rush of ecstasy. The grammar of this addiction is devastatingly simple: "I want **that** right now." The **"that"** in question (image, organ, fetish, whip) tantalizes us with the hope of pleasure or release from tension . . . but (we knew it all along) it leads inexorably, after orgasm, to panic and shame, an increase in tension, and the desire to act out. And this scenario goes on repeating itself again and again in empty, debilitating rituals.

Like other addictions, sex addiction comes to us unbidden and unheralded; we find that we are afflicted without remembering how or when or why. Often sex addiction invades our lives in our earliest years because of neglect or punishment, or as a result of seductive behavior in our family of origin or outright sexual abuse at the hands of other children or adults. And we often go on re-enacting scenarios of exploitation and humiliation (which we originally hated and feared) without knowing what we are seeking or why.

Healthy human sexuality implies dynamic, living relationships—with ourselves and others. It includes the embrace of tolerance and affection, where we can feel at ease and confident and, ultimately, at home. Working against this vital energy, sex addiction drives us into lonely and desperate places where there is no such thing as a relationship, let alone love. We experience long stretches of loneliness and pain, and the dark night of despair.

At some point we lost our bearings and our sense of boundaries. Sex has become murky, entangling, and wounding. We seek to gratify ourselves through a rush of euphoria associated with images or bodies divorced from wholeness and love—only to find ourselves, in the cold aftermath of our longed-for pleasure, bereft of any sense of integrity and self-worth. We need to come back from these destructive and perilous places. It is urgent for us to keep creating new selves and choosing new directions.

To do this, we need to re-connect with ourselves and with others and get back into living touch and tenderness. We can make these vital contacts in therapy, in groups, and in Twelve Step programs. Twelve Step programs for sex addicts offer the promise of openness, a step-by-step process of recovery, and a community of support and love. Those of us who are sex addicts need others to help us move beyond ourselves, to break out of our isolation and our shame. It is only with others that we can learn to be trusting and unafraid, and get our bearings again in healthy relationships.

We also need to get back in touch with ourselves. All of us, as human beings marked by our culture, carry on inner conversations of many voices, some kindly and supportive, others filled with accusations and abuse (*"you are lazy, worthless, dirty, shameful, crazy"*). These voices in us come from afar, from our childhoods and even beyond: perhaps our parents heard them and spoke them, and their parents too. In many cases, our own unique voices were stolen from us and silenced; what ran through our heads was a chorus of criticism and recrimination coming from outside. These other, alien voices gradually became engraved in us, scripted into us, often without our knowledge. They too easily go on repeating their shattering, soul-destroying messages like record-players out of control (*"lazy, worthless, dirty, shameful, crazy"*).

This book offers other voices and other scripts. Each passage in this book is a conversation taking place among the various voices that speak inside us. In the main body of the passage, it is mostly the first-person voice that is heard, as if we were speaking out loud our most intimate thoughts. Many tones and messages give color to this first-person voice, just as "I" am made up of a variety of actors, emotions, and experiences. This "I" voice can be a whining child, a self-centered egoist, a smooth-talking hypocrite, a seductive Don Juan. After a while, it may become rational, calm, even serene. Then, suddenly the addict breaks in; now the voice is perverse, obsessive, and full of the clamor and melancholia of unrequited love. Later, we may be surprised to hear it speaking of kindly feelings, generous acts, and even heroic deeds.

In the pages that follow, this "I" voice articulates our thoughts and feelings as richly complex men and women and as addicts struggling towards recovery. And then, at the end of each passage, and sometimes during the passage itself, we speak back to ourselves, sometimes in the old hostile, shaming voice, but sometimes in a new, positive, healthy way. This second, italicized voice is the *"**you**"* voice which, especially for addicts, is often the accusing, hating part of ourselves. It is initially a monolithic voice, and it comes from uncomprehending or hostile parents or adults or society in general (*"you are lazy, worthless, dirty, shameful, crazy"*). Many of us incorporate other people's disapproval into ourselves; as children especially, we become scared and scarred by scripts that bite deeply into us with messages of contempt. They rage at us ceaselessly, especially in times of stress, when we are most in need of the support of rational discourse.

Gradually, as our program of recovery takes hold, we learn to modify this hostility and speak back to ourselves more kindly and calmly. As the days pass, the exchanges between the "I" and "*you*" become less strident. There are relapses, sometimes brutal and shocking, as the old hateful, jarring self-division suddenly threatens to split us asunder again. Then we hear again, in agony, those voices that terrify and humiliate us, and we need all our courage to keep moving on. But throughout this book, as in our recovery, the overall movement is always, and vigorously, towards inner harmony and peace.

Many of us still hear contemptuous voices that shatter our confidence and keep us shackled back in infantilism and shame. As we recover from our addiction, we find that the messages of these voices are every day less potent. Moreover, as we strive to change our destructive voices and affirm our new selves, we quicken our own recovery.

Our voices become voices of healing, voices of strength.

In this way, we work towards a modification and, ultimately, a reconciliation of the many voices within us; and we confirm our growing sense that we can love—and that we are, with all our human faults and frailties, worth being loved, after all.

So I hope that these texts will help to move us forward to a loving reconciliation with ourselves and with the splendor of the world that embraces us.

—P. Williamson

Editor's Note

Editors are supposed to stand aloof, detached and analytical, in order to bring critical objectivity to the book's completion. As my work with P. Williamson ends, however, I want to step out of that role and express my admiration for the author and the people who have inspired these dialogues.

I began this work at a considerable distance, imagining the voices to represent Otherness, people who had nothing to do with me, whose lives and experience must be foreign to my own. With every reading, however, their insights have further enriched my life. As each revision cut closer to the bone, I felt joyous, thrilled by this book's courage. I began to see myself and Williamson's throng as brothers and sisters in the human family. All of us house a judge like the author's italicized voices in the back closets of our minds. All of us struggle to transcend the harmful influences we bring from childhood. We can all appreciate the valor required by such confrontations in the darkest reaches of the self.

Other Voices, Other Scripts has inspirited me. To P. Williamson and all who speak here and who read this book: I wish you well in your journey.

—J.R.T.

The promise of new beginnings

As the world turns and the New Year opens, I welcome the challenge of new beginnings. My life keeps pace with the movement of the world where change is the law of life.

My addiction has caused strife and loneliness and grief. I need to keep working on my recovery and make amends to myself and others.

Sex has been a weapon and a snare for me; I have hurt other people and enmeshed myself in compulsive acting out. Empty rituals became a substitute for living.

It is time to affirm my desire and need to change. I am determined to open myself to the world and bring my sexuality into a more human, loving place.

You seem ready to continue and renew yourself as the New Year starts. I used to demean you and assault you with the voice of an angry parent. Now I feel closer to you and more at ease. I've a hunch we're going to get along better this year.

1

January 2
Own voice

As a woman, I never realized how many of the voices I listened to were not my own. And it got even worse when my mother died, as if she had come and set up housekeeping in my head.

Yes, really. It was like having a permanent guest in the back bedroom, one who never found anything to be happy about. "The living-room floor, dear, it needs waxing again," "Do you really still need to work—what about the children and Jack, darling?" "Aren't you just a little bit too old for all that sex, now?" "Just look at that sink, really. . . . "

It was driving me crazy. Then I talked to some women in my group who heard the same kinds of things, all day long, and especially in bed. They all had these voices in their heads. "That's not nice, dear," "Shame on you," "He did **what**?"

So we recorded some of the craziest voices and then played them back and listened . . . and smiled and then laughed and laughed.

That was a tonic, I can tell you.

Yes, you bet it was. It helped me, too, just to hear the kinds of things I'd been repeating all these years. My ears were burning, but really I couldn't stop laughing at myself, in the end. Nothing like laughter for letting in some fresh air.

For many years I've looked at people's bodies, including my own, as sites of sexual exploitation.

My own body used to be a place where I sought only self-gratification. And I reduced other people's bodies to bits and pieces—zones and organs of pleasure, fractured images that inspired gaze and lust, outside any human relationship.

Now I am learning to see my body as a place for love and intimacy. I don't abuse it or use it as an instrument of exploitation masquerading as affection.

These days I don't leer at women as they pass by or gaze at pornographic pictures—those infantile pictures where bodies are cut up into fragments and pasted into images that evoke sensuality divorced from touch and tenderness.

I am learning to see the human body as a source of energy and delight.

> *It's been hard to change, but you are changing each day. I feel better about myself, too, and kinder. What's happening?*

We're learning to be human.

January 4
Dialogue

I feel like a child. I want to get high, act out, run away.

> *Go on then. Do it! That's all you are really, a spoiled child. Take what you want—but I'll make you pay for it. I always do.*

I know. I feel you hovering over me, just like my dad. You're always there, scolding, sneering, waiting for me to make a slip.

> *And you always do make a slip, don't you, you worthless little creep!*

Wait. I don't need to sit and listen to that tired old bullying voice of yours. I'm beginning to take care of myself and reach out and get help when I want to act out. People in my group are there for me now. And I'm learning to be there for myself.

> *We'll see. You certainly are stronger and braver these days.*

Yes, and I'm not afraid of you anymore, Big Daddy. Why not try to act as equals and have a real dialogue?

> *Equals? Well, I don't know about that. I'll have to think about it. I will think about it. Maybe we can both change. What do you think?*

I just told you what I think. Why don't you listen?

> *I'm sorry. I need to change my habits, too, don't I?*

I talked in group today. Did my First Step.

I'd written it all out. I was scared. I kept my eyes on the page and waited. My face felt frozen.

We started the meeting. Did the business stuff.

Someone came in late. There was a pause. The woman next to me whispered: "Hi. I know it's hard, but why don't you just say it? Just talk."

I looked up and saw the others smiling at me in a friendly way. I could feel the support.

I put the paper down and looked up.

I couldn't speak. I couldn't say it.

The woman next to me gave my arm a squeeze.

I burst into tears. They waited, smiling.

I said, "Hi, my name is Anne, and I'm a sex addict."

You were so brave. It was great. It's hard to break the ice. I was scared, too, and that sometimes makes me want to terrorize you. But this time we made it, together.

January 6
Inner child

Are you there, old man?

> *Yes. Just dozing a bit, that's all.*

I need to ask you something. What's this inner child they're always talking about?

> *It's the real you, before you became an addict.*

Where is it?

> *It's there inside you.*

What happened to it?

> *That's a good question. What do you think happened?*

It got lost. Buried alive.

> *Exactly. Buried alive beneath your addiction and your shame.*

But it's still there, isn't it? That's what they mean when they say we can "return to sanity."

> *Yes, that's it. But not just sanity—spontaneity, energy, feelings, openness, faith.*

Sounds like life, to me.

> *You're right. It is life.*

I look in the mirror and see a strangely familiar face which nods and winks and frowns and smiles. Is that me? Is that how other people see me? Is that really me?

Do I look like that every day? Is this the once-and-for-all real me?

Maybe there isn't a moment when I can say once and for all, "That's me." Perhaps the "I" that sees and speaks is always a little bit distant from the "You" in the mirror—and both are always changing, too.

But that interplay could be fun, even an adventure, because it means I'm in a relationship with myself that is full of change and surprises.

Yes, that's true. And don't forget I'm here, too—Old Supervoice that used to be always scolding and bullying. Now I'm changing, too!

January 8
Head first

The trouble with intellectuals like you is that you're always generalizing.

That sounds like a pretty good generalization to me.

>*It must be catching.*

And a good thing, too. We need to have some adult conversation around here. In the group all we do is talk from the gut.

>*Isn't that what we need to do?*

That's what they **say** we need, but you and I know better. We need to put the head first.

>*Because we're intellectuals?*

Yes. And because the gut can't generalize.

>*But that's precisely the point. The gut is where your feelings are, and your feelings are what got all mixed up. And you are you, not a generalization.*

In my addiction, you mean?

>*Yes. And your shame.*

And I can't generalize about my shame?

>*Not if you want to get well.*

I do.

>*Fine. We can take it from there and get down to the "nitty gritty."*

That's a fine phrase for an intellectual!

>*But that's where the work starts, Socrates!*

For a long time I felt alienated and even proud to be different and alone.

I didn't realize how isolated I was until I really needed help and had nobody to turn to. My life fell apart like a house of cards.

A friend recommended a group for sex addicts. I thought it was a crazy idea but I went along to please him.

I was terrified. I'd been alone so long. I hardly even knew how to talk openly to other people.

Gradually I felt at ease. I made new friends there. They made me feel wanted and loved for the person I am. They even hugged me—**me**, an addict!

I feel more and more at home. It's a new community—a community of real people who are bound to one another by threads of love as strong as steel.

> *I remember your fear. I took advantage of it to remind you how lonely and worthless you were.*

You made things worse, far worse.

> *And now?*

You're getting better—we both are.

> *Trust me.*

Give me time.

January 10
Signs

I felt like acting out this morning.

> *What happened?*

Nothing. Nothing special. But I had bad dreams, and I woke up feeling restless. My eye was twitching a bit, and I knew my irritation could explode into anger if I didn't watch it.

> *And from anger to acting out. . .*

. . . is only one short step.

> *But you did read the signs.*

Yes, that's it. In the past, I was half-asleep, half-addicted. I never really knew what was going on inside me. But now I say, "Wait a minute, Sally, something's going on. There's a red flag flying at the masthead, and it's not the Stars and Stripes."

> *Red for danger.*

Yes, and red for anger. That's what used to trip me up and send me spinning into my addiction.

> *I'm glad you're reading the signs now.*

Yes—and learning to read myself.

> *I like that idea . . . maybe we're texts as well as people,*
> *pages of signs that make up our personal histories.*
> *And recovery is learning to read!*

As a child I always heard the same messages: "You'll never be like your brother." "You just don't measure up." "We're disappointed in you." "You're a failure."

And the messages hardened into scripts and became engraved in stone.

I lost confidence in myself. I had no core of beliefs to sustain me. Whenever I wanted to try something new, I always felt those negative scripts working in me, promising only failure, beating me up.

So I withdrew into a private world of sexual fantasies. I stole my dad's pornography and sought pleasure in images and in my own body. Masturbation became my solace and my secret shame.

And always those harsh voices and those hateful scripts engraved in stone!

It was only after I joined a group and heard other voices—warm, kind, supportive—that I began to feel wanted and confident.

Now I don't have to listen to those old voices anymore. I'm creating a new script for my own life.

It's been hard for you, I know. And of course I was enjoying myself playing all those voices and watching you suffer. But now you're getting strong and sane, I don't have the power anymore. And you know what? I don't even want it!

January 12
Adulthood

How come I always think of you as older?

> *Maybe because I'm wiser.*

Give me a break! Until recently you were just as flaky as I was, but you hid it behind all that adult bluster. Mm, I suppose I think of you as older because you've taken on so many of the voices and messages of grandparents and parents.

> *Now you're calling me an old fogey!*

You certainly weren't a kind old fogey. You waited until I was completely engrossed in my addiction, and then you'd start ranting and raving about degeneracy and madness and on and on. You were a mixture of the absent landlord and the omnipresent tyrant.

> *I sound awful. Was I really that bad?*

Yes, you were. But since we joined that group, you've toned down a lot. You're becoming a friend, you know. Is that hard for you?

> *I'm touched! I only knew how to make you scared and keep your distance. Now you're so much stronger, life is going to be fun. I'll try not to say "I told you so!"*

12

I was such a neat little good little girl, I was almost invisible in the family. I was the one who hung around, taken for granted.

But I wanted to be loved and not tolerated, hanging around on the edge. So I gave myself to the first boy who wanted sex with me, and I never looked back.

When I was sad—sex. When I was lonely—sex. When I was hurt—sex. That was how I sought comfort and recognition.

But I found only pain and loneliness and disgust. My body was just an instrument, a plaything, not a vital part of me.

I split off from myself just as I split off from the family. And it goes on and on.

Will I never find love, real, honest, open, carefree love?

> *I don't think you will. You're too selfish, too wrapped up in yourself. And that makes you an easy target for all those old tapes and voices.*

I'm not down and out, you know. Don't think you're always going to have the last word.

January 14
Beliefs

I grew up believing that I was never going to amount to much. In my head was always a voice telling me that I was useless and bad.

A failure! Weak! Unlovable! Dirty! Untrustworthy! Clumsy! Evil!

I shriveled up into my shell and sought to find some power and release in sex. At least there I could enjoy the illusion that I was in control and could escape other people's scorn.

I turned to sex whenever I felt lonely or angry or full of fear—and of course my sex life became lonely and angry and full of fear.

It took many years of misery to convince myself that sex was not the answer.

Sex had become the problem.

> *You were in a bad way, and of course I took advantage of that.*
>
> *I convinced you that you were worthless and evil. How easy it was to go on being the vindictive parent!*

I gave away my power—to you and to my addiction.

> *But now you're changing; we both are.*

Yes. Changing beliefs can help us change our lives.

> *I believe that, too.*

About that penis of yours. . . .

What about it?

> *It's faulty.*

You sound like a plumber.

> *This is serious. Last night when you were talking to Mrs. Peterson, it was, well, prominent.*

That's because I was thinking of Joanie.

> *Why were you thinking of Joanie when you were talking to Mrs. Peterson?*

Have you looked at Mrs. Peterson lately?

> *Handsome is as handsome does, you know.*

I've never understood that expression.

> *And there's another thing. Were you thinking of Mrs. Peterson when you were with Joanie last night?*

No. Why do you ask?

> *Because, well . . .*

Well, what?

> *The plumbing didn't work, did it?*

It seems to have a life of its own.

> *Isn't that because it's not integrated into your life? You've detached yourself from it, just as you're detached from sex. Detached, yet addicted. That's something we need to heal, together.*

January 16
Phone-in

What I used to love was those really intimate, sexy phone calls . . . with complete strangers.

I'd pour myself a drink, make myself really comfortable, turn out the lights . . . and with a touch of the finger the magic ritual began.

Hours later I'd wake up from the trance and somehow I always felt cheated, and a lot poorer.

I was looking for something but found nothing except another voice speaking about another empty life.

I was scared to talk about this in the group for a long time; it seemed so demeaning, so inhuman.

Then another person owned this kind of behavior, and everyone listened calmly and supportively.

And a voice said, "We have phone-ins here, you know. Here's a list. When you feel lonely, give us a call."

Now I phone in every day, and I hear on the other end of the wire a strong, responsive, caring voice.

The voice of sanity and love.

Of course, I could have told you so. But I was so busy being the punishing parent that I didn't have time for any kind words. It's good to hear you talking sense now. And it certainly makes sense to me, too.

16

I sit here and worry and twitch. I feel like acting out.

> *Take it easy now. You have options, you know.*

Name some.

> *You can phone someone in the group, go for a walk, play with the dog, turn on some music, stand on your head, talk to me.*

I don't know how to stand on my head.

> *Smart ass! Change direction, make choices—you know what I mean.*

Get some energy and some focus.

> *Exactly. You've got it. In the old days you'd have been acting out already.*

Yes, that's true. I'd have zoomed in on my addiction. Sleazy close-ups of the addict at hard labor!

> *And I'd have been egging you on, then beating you up.*

Right. It just goes to show that we can change. And I want to.

> *New voices open up other worlds, you know. Words prompt actions and create new patterns.*

It's good to hear you talking like this.

> *And you?*

I feel like shouting out to the world: "I'm creating my own voice at last."

January 18
Sadness

"You're a really sweet girl, you know"—and the eyes of my uncle are taking off my blouse.

"I'd love to have you come and baby-sit for me one night, you know when my wife goes to visit her folks"—and the neighbor's little squeeze on my knee.

"Of course, nice girls like you don't have any vices"—and the thick little chuckle and the leer from Dad's best friend.

And Dad? He was away most of the time, and even when he was at home, it was as if I didn't exist. It was Jamie, Jamie, Jamie.

I got the message. I let my uncle take me to his cabin in the woods and do what his eyes had promised. I knew it was wrong but I didn't care. He had a sweet face, and there was a kind of sick thrill in doing it, and a sadness for me that won't go away.

Ever.

I feel for you and want to help. Please don't push me away this time. We can overcome this sadness if we work together. It helps to be in the group and to talk. I really am on your side, you know. We need each other.

18

I feel down these days.

> *Try saying your affirmations out loud.*

That sounds silly. I'd be too embarrassed!

> *I don't mean on the bus, silly goose. At home, in your own room.*

What's the point, then?

> *To change gears, change words, change ideas, change feelings.*

Can words help?

> *They can hurt, you stupid little girl.*

Ouch! I see what you mean.

> *And they can soothe you, like the sea, and bring you strength and energy, like the wind, and make you feel loved and lovable—as you are and as you should be, and as you will be . . . now and always.*

Oh, that sounds so good. Please say it again.

> *You say it . . . that's right. Feel good? And then we learn to say Yes to life, and each day really is a new beginning!*

Yes, it is. Yes.

January 20
Unlovable

As a child I hated being thin and pale and weak. I would look in the mirror and dream of having a different body, bronzed and strong.

I sought out other men who were like my dream, and I wanted to be like them, and then I wanted to have them.

For years I wandered in a desert of lust, seeking anonymous encounters in books and magazines, in love with the perfect image, the perfect stranger.

Finally a friend caught me coming out of a porno bookstore. Luckily, he had been on that suffering path, too. So he took me with him to his group, and made me feel wanted and welcome.

Now I have friends who are not supermen but human and caring. I love them not for their image but for themselves.

> *How I remember those dreadful days and nights, cruising after illusions. And I was always there, of course, egging you on and then punishing you.*

Talk about double binds!

> *I know. But now there are new **bonds** between us.*

I'm working on my First Step, you know the one that says our lives have become unmanageable and we are powerless over our addiction.

I don't see it that way, myself. I mean, I work hard every day at the office, and I certainly think I deserve some fun after eight hours a day buying and selling houses. I go to the bar for a drink with the other women, and then they go off home to husband and the kids. I stay around and have a couple more drinks. Then I join another group for just a few more drinks . . . .

It's true I usually don't go home alone. But you can get tired of going home to the same old place and opening another can of soup. Not even a cat for company.

I like being sociable. I'm fun. Nothing weird. Good clean sex. It's part of life, too, you know. Must have some fun.

Yes, I'm often late for work. I missed a promotion last month. Friends? Well, let's see. You know I kind of like being alone.

Alone. Alone. Alone.

> *I feel that you want to talk yourself away from self-knowledge. But we both know that it doesn't make sense to keep on hiding. The group does help. . . you've said so several times. Let's keep working on that First Step.*

It's hard.

> *It's worth it.*

January 22
Hippos

Sex can be really funny, you know. All that breathing and blushing and blotches.

> *Blotches?*

You know, on my body when I'm getting excited and he's puffing and panting away like an old train.

> *Yes, I know. He really works at it doesn't he, just like his jogging. You, too, by the way.*

Writhing and moaning and twitching around. It's quite loony, really. Suppose the neighbors saw?

> *They'd have a good laugh, too, you know.*

Would they?

> *I'm sure they would. I saw them once in the bath together, like a pair of hippos.*

Hippos or hippies?

> *Hippos, honest. They do it too, you know.*

I sometimes feel that the so-called sexual revolution turned our whole culture into a sexual bazaar. If you weren't doing it madly, all the time, you felt left out in the cold.

So I rushed about and slept around and felt I was really with it . . . until I realized that actually I was without it, without a sense of value in my sexual life.

In my group, we don't just sit around and talk about sex. We try to work out for ourselves what it means to have a good and healthy sex life.

It has nothing to do with quantity or gender or heterosexuality or homosexuality. It has to do with how I feel and act and interact with others.

Sex needs a loving embrace, a ring of bright love that we create out of affection and trust.

Good for you. And good for me, too. I can see trust and love coming into our relationship, too. We need that—both of us.

January 24
Duo

I really think I'm going crazy.

> *No, you are crazy! You were always the insane one in the family, remember, hiding in the closet?*

You made me feel crazy, all of you. You set me up and kept me outside, always outside the family, an outcast.

> *That was your fault, your fault, your fault. You were useless and loathsome, always locked away in your room, reading that glossy filth.*

What can I do?

> *Nothing. You're damned.*

You're wrong, you know. Don't forget the Program. I'm not going to go under. I'm feeling new strength, new faith, new courage. I've got real friends now, and hope.

> *You'll never make it; don't even try.*

Sorry, this time you're wrong. I know I'm on the way home.

> *It's going to be a rough road, you know.*

I'm not afraid.

> *That's true. I feel your strength.*

Let's journey together, shall we?

> *Let's try. Let's work. Let's live!*

I blocked out my earliest years until recently. Then in therapy I remembered . . .

. . . the woman in black, the woman of my nightmares . . . my mother away in the hospital . . . the pins . . . the dark closet . . . the cold, closed face . . . the pain.

I shut myself off in the closet of my addiction. I never trusted a single adult.

My father knew about my aunt's sadistic behavior, didn't he? She hated men and she hated boys.

They were all the same, those adults, cowards or tyrants.

It wasn't until I came into a group for sex addiction that I ever trusted a single human being. I was amazed on the first day to hear some guy talk about incest with his mother, compulsive masturbation, sex in public toilets—and then everyone gathered round and hugged him!

It's taken me three years of my adult life working in a group to get back what I needed and deserved as a child—the bond of love.

But I've found it.

More power to you and the group and your Higher Power. I hated it too, being always on the outside, sneering and jeering. I admire your courage; it helps me change, too.

January 26
Blindness

As a sex addict, I was blind to the complexity and difference of other people. I worshiped images and icons that let me live in a closed-off dream world.

I wanted everything to be simple so that I could be in control. So I acted out with pictures and fantasies that were secret and safe.

I would get angry if my husband made demands on me or asserted his freedom.

Now I am in a group where I am learning to open my eyes to the particularity of others.

I don't lust for static images anymore. I am beginning to love real, dynamic people.

> *Yes, I see what you mean. You really were blind to everything except the things that gave you the illusion of security.*

Yes, I was blind. But not anymore. Let's open our eyes and live!

Why doesn't someone see me, take some notice?

> *Because you're just a little mouse, that's why.*

That's it. Make things worse, King Rat.

> *I don't need to make things worse. You're doing a fine job yourself, dragging yourself down into the slime. You'll never get out, you know. So you might just as well go on acting out.*

Thanks a lot. I hear you, and I know you're expecting me to run away into fantasy and then the ritual and then . . .

> *. . . the acting out, the act. Go on, why not.*

I'll tell you why not. Because I can see the end from here—more misery, more shame, more thoughts of killing myself or killing you.

> *Same thing.*

True. But I choose not to. I'm going to get on the phone and then tonight go to my group and keep on following the Twelve Step way. It works, and you know it.

> *We'll see. Sometimes I think you're right, but it's going to be painful, all that change. Why not wait a little? After all, you're still young. Enjoy yourself!*

January 28
Head trip

I think I'm getting to understand the nature of addiction.

> *Whose?*

Addiction in general, and sex addiction in particular.

> *Yours?*

Well, I'm more interested in the theory of it, you know, family systems, and trauma, and repression, and that sort of thing.

> *Very smart. Does it help you?*

Well, it will.

> *When?*

Eventually. I mean, I think it will. At least it should, shouldn't it?

> *Sure it's important to have insight, but insight into your own real, specific, everyday life and the part addiction plays in it. The Program isn't an intellectual exercise, it's a way of changing your life, starting right now. Does that sound a bit preachy? It's true, for me anyway.*

I'm listening. Go on. I like this new voice of yours.

I had this relationship with a guy from my office. I knew he had a reputation as a Don Juan, so I was on my guard.

He noticed me one day in the restaurant. Came over and chatted. The next day he wrote me a funny note. Then flowers. A movie. A surprise picnic. Promises. Bed.

We had great sex, lots of laughs, a couple of long weekends together. I was fond of him. He was very attentive. Sincere. Charming. Suddenly I was in love, desperately.

One day, after dinner at my place, with the candles still flickering, I suggested we should spend our winter vacation together skiing—we were in love, weren't we? As I was talking, I saw him nudge back his cuff and take a quick glance at his watch. In that tiny gesture I saw the end.

I was right as usual.

———————————

I don't want to beat on you, my dear, but you might almost say you were wrong as usual, wrong from the beginning. I think you're addicted to charming, shallow men. We need help. And there are programs for just this kind of thing—for people who love and lose . . . and lose and lose.

January 30
Performance

Many men and women sex addicts get high on the feeling that they're "really good in bed." By "good" of course they mean "great," "fantastic," "out of this world."

What's wrong with this world? Everything—for those of us who can find meaning only in sexual performance. It's because we really hate ourselves and the reality of our everyday lives that we build up our false selves through sexual exploits and exploitation.

I need to get feedback on this. In my group people listen and help me move forward, away from such silly ideas as "out of this world" and "performance." They take me seriously (they've been there too); and then they help me do what's necessary.

They teach me, gently, to laugh at myself.

> *Well, that's something new! You took yourself dead seriously, and that made it easy for me. If one of your partners didn't give you an A plus, I'd have some fun at your expense.*

Yes. You didn't help. You were so sarcastic and superior, the Big Professor.

> *But not anymore.*

No. Not anymore.

*L*et's have a talk, shall we?

I'm not here.

> *What's going on?*

I'm not myself.

> *What are you? Where are you?*

An addict. In my addiction.

> *We can still talk, can't we?*

No. My addiction takes me out of myself. And that's what I crave sometimes, when I just can't bear to be me.

> *How can I reach you, then?*

You can't, when I'm like this.

> *Let me try. Let me in.*

I'm out.

> *That's spooky. Out? How can we be intimate if you're not there? How can you be intimate with yourself, if you're not there?*

You tell me. You know everything.

> *Can't we work on this together?*

No. Not today. I told you. I'm out.

February 1
Boundaries

When I was a child I felt strange messages coming to me about sex. There was a lot of nudity in the house and with it inappropriate glances and gestures.

I didn't feel my body was my own. My brothers and sisters were always touching me and getting me aroused in spite of myself.

Sex was without permission, without boundaries, without consent. Sex was coercion and aggression, not choice.

My acting out was a repetition of that world of trespass and victimization. It took me ages to get back my sense of limits and my own freedom.

My Program is giving me the power to own my sexuality and the courage to call it my own.

> *Sure, I remember those days. You really were a victim and that made it easy for me to be your executioner!*

And you enjoyed that, didn't you?

> *Yes, I did. But not anymore, though.*

Do you miss it?

> *Sometimes. Well, not really.*

Sure?

> *Sure.*

In Sunday School I learned that my body is a sacred vessel, pure and waiting to be filled.

I loved that idea. It was real. I could see the shape and the color of it in my mind's eye. Like a Greek vase.

I asked the nun who was teaching the class what the vessel was waiting to be filled with. She said, "The Holy Spirit."

"When?"

"When you're married," she said.

"Can't it be filled outside marriage?"

"No."

I loved that, too. I felt holy.

Then we learned about Eve and the lust in her body and the serpent and Original Sin and degradation and touching yourself "down there" and hell and damnation and the fire that burned in you for ever and ever.

I masturbated all through my teens and I still do, often.

I'm scared, even now.

> *I really do feel your pain and your fear. But at least now we can talk about it.*

I'm still scared.

> *So am I. But we can learn to talk our way out of those myths!*

February 3
Crazy talk

Just once more. I need it. It doesn't hurt anyone. I can't stand the tension. I want the thrill. I need the release.

> *You fool. You're worthless. Outcast. Scum.*

But I want it. I can't bear the pain. Let me go, just this once.

> *Go, then, and be damned. Go and get lost. That's all you deserve.*

Hold it. Steady. Let's remember the group, the warmth, the love, the power.

> *Hold on, yes, steady. Keep faith, keep to the path, move forward.*

Love is the way, the new power.

> *Yes, it used to be like that—the cacophony of voices, the madness, the war. Always restless, tormented, chaotic. Then came the new power from the group; hope, love, peace, and the search for serenity.*

Now you're talking sense again!

Addictive sexual excitement is a feeling without an object. It's like being all dressed up with nowhere to go.

First the feeling of emptiness, the void. Then the ritual—images, fantasies, clothes, mirror, make-up. And then?

I hesitate, absent-minded. **What** was it I wanted? **Where** was I going? Ah, yes, of course, **that** was it.

But what was **that**? And was it really that?

And where **was** it?

And after that, what?

A friend of mine shook me up by saying that sex addiction is a sickness of a very particular kind—an eroticized homesickness.

An eroticized homesickness with no hope and no home.

But now in my group I'm finding hope and strength to go forward.

> *You're right on target today! You're really leaping ahead in this Twelve Step Program. It's sometimes hard for me to keep up. Please be patient with your one-time parent!*

One day at a time, old man.

February 5
Glass house

I do fairly well, on the whole. I mean, people like me, and
I'm good at my job. I've just moved into a new apartment and
I've got a nice car—one of those Japanese ones that are safe
and easy to drive.

I take care of my health and do a bit of exercise once or twice
a week. I read and watch television and call Mom every
evening.

I looked in the mirror this morning. I'm still young and quite
pretty really, if I do say so myself. I eat carefully and watch
my weight. Men don't like fat women these days.

Men don't like me much, either. We go out once, and that's it.
I don't understand it. I still look young, as I said. And I'm
good at my job. And I've got this car, as I told you. It's one of
those Japanese ones that are safe and easy to drive. I still call
Mom every evening. I talk most of the time, but she listens,
she really does.

What will I do when she dies?

---

*I think we need to talk, you and I. It's time I spoke up. I
think you're getting addicted to yourself—all that
talking and talking. And then you are nibbling
something all the time. And what about all those sexy
pictures you take to bed with you? We need to talk and
get some help.*

I'd watch my dad and see how he did things. I wanted to look like him, be him.

> *Why?*

He was Dad.

> *Did you want to be him or be like him?*

How do you mean?

> *When he read the newspaper, you'd hold your book, just like him. Remember? You'd look the same.*

Yes, that's what I wanted.

> *Did you want to look like Dad or learn to read, like Dad?*

Mm. I think I see what you mean. Go on.

> *I mean, did you want to do exactly what he was doing because he was doing it, or learn to do something for you, for yourself?*

I think I was confused. Identification and imitation, they're different, aren't they?

> *Yes.*

If I just imitate, then there's no me there. And I want to be me.

> *That's it. That's what acting out is—wanting to be someone or something, without lapse or gap. It's the gap between people that makes the difference. Does this make sense? Can we work on it?*

37

February 7
Taking over

When I was a girl, I always wanted to please people. I was very observant, and I anticipated people's needs—I'd get the Kleenex or find the ashtray or take away the glass or the coffee cup.

I even finished people's sentences for them. I was so attuned to what was going on that when someone was talking to me, I knew how the words were going to come out, so I said them, triumphantly, with a little smile.

Last summer my uncle was telling me about a sailing trip. I like him, and I was hanging on his words. As he got to the scary part in the storm, I guessed what was coming and took the words out of his mouth.

He laughed and asked me, with a smile, what it felt like to be afraid most of the time. I nearly stopped breathing! He put his arm around me, and I sobbed like a child.

He talked to me a lot that summer and gave me a phone number just before he left. It was a local sex addiction group, just exactly what I needed.

How did he know?

> *Because he loves you and love has second sight. And you did rather give yourself away—always finishing people's sentences so you wouldn't be caught off guard! If we continue to help each other, we can learn to speak in our own voices.*

My own voice. What's that?

> *You'll find it. You'll **create** it!*

38

I feel only half alive.

> *That means you're half dead.*

That's typical of you.

> *What do you want?*

Kindness. Just ordinary human kindness.

> *You'll get it when you deserve it.*

Dammit. That's all I hear from you—bribing, blackmailing, carping, sniping, bullying. I'm fed up with your tone, your voice, your existence.

> *I'm here for good, you know. Yours for life!*

I hate life. I hate you.

> *That's what I like to hear. Power!*

Power! It's tyranny. And you know it.

> *Yes, I know it, and I love it. You've put yourself in chains, you stupid little addict. All those promises, and then the acting out. But I'm not complaining: that's exactly how I like things.*

February 9
Getting along

Everyone was ambitious in our family. That was just the way
it was.

Joe became a doctor, Giles went into the army, like Dad, and
Mary is at law school. I know that happens in lots of families,
but in our family it happened right from the very beginning
and every single day. It was always happening and nobody
took time off to live.

Except me. I was the odd one out, and the funny thing is that
it was okay. It was as if the Perfect Family could function only
in opposition to an underlying craziness. So I was allowed,
even encouraged, to be irresponsible and crazy.

They liked that. They left me alone.

They abandoned me, and yet they needed me.

That's how it was and that's how I got hooked on dope and
sex.

They made me feel crazy and I became crazy.

Simple.

----

*That's really how it was, but I've never seen it that way
until now. I was too busy babying you along to realize
how isolated you were getting. And then all that sex to
try and make contact. It breaks my heart. But we can
work on it—not for them, for us.*

I do get strength from therapy and from working in the group, but still . . .

> *Not enough?*

Exactly. And anyway, I can't spend my life in therapy!

> *No. I suppose not. Well, what else is there?*

That's the point. What else **is** there?

> *There's us.*

But we're the problem not the solution!

> *No, we're **part** of the solution.*

Which part?

> *Our healthy part. The part that keeps talking and thinking and feeling healthy thoughts. The part that can have this conversation, for example.*

Clever! I never thought of that. It's true we can talk to each other these days—maybe we can talk each other back to sanity!

> *You laugh, but there's a lot in what you say.*

I agree. And you're getting to be quite a wise old bird yourself, dear Supervoice!

February 11
Fault line

"Let's go out on a drive. I'll let you take the wheel." How jolly my uncle was, always thinking up new tricks for his favorite nephew. He introduced me to sailing, to horses, to baseball, to everything connected with the outdoor life.

And to sex.

That day, as I was driving, concentrating like any fourteen-year-old on the road ahead, I felt his hand playing with me . . . down there. I didn't stop. He kept on smiling and joking about the car, and anyway, I hate to say it, but I kind of liked the feeling.

It was only afterwards that I saw in the contracting pupils of his eyes, behind his thick, clumsy glasses, my own fear and his shame. It's strange: I felt bad for **him**, and even, in a way, guilty.

Perhaps he was trying to be friendly . . . and I had led him on, till he lost control. I knew about the demon sex, from Mom. And, after all, I never told him to stop.

And the pleasure, the rush, the fear, the shame, the clumsy glasses, and that lonely man. I couldn't get it straight.

It's taken me fifteen years to get it straight.

> *Yes, it's been lonely and you've been brave. How could you talk about it . . . and yet how could you understand it until you **did** talk about it? That's why I bless this group of ours, this place where we can leave our shame and confusion behind.*

And learn to be ourselves.

You know I like plays where there's sadness and tragedy and then along comes the fool or the clown who makes us laugh.

Me too. It helps take us out of ourselves.

It's not that, exactly. We're still ourselves, but laughter gives us another perspective.

Does that help with addiction, too?

I think so, yes. I once went off to California pursuing a stud I adored and who'd turned me down, and I lost my luggage at the airport, had my wallet stolen, got diarrhea, and had to sleep in a flophouse with fleas in the bed and the other women cursing and shouting all night long.

Heavens! And that made you laugh?

Not at the time! But now it seems comic—all that High Romance, Tragic Passion . . . and then those bedbugs.

Sounds as if you had the bedbug yourself in those days, my dear.

Exactly. I think I got just what I was asking for!

Yes. There is something comic about sex addiction—all that rushing and lusting and straining and obsessing. And those damned bedbugs! It's good to laugh together, isn't it?

Yes. Laughter can get rid of the bedbug!

February 13
Repetition

What am I looking for when I go and act out? I can't even say, and yet I still do it.

*What **are** you looking for?*

I'm looking for . . . that whatever-it-is-that-takes-me-out-of-myself.

Where do you go?

Down into a dream. And there, what do I find? Loneliness and shame. But there's something I want in those sexual encounters, something I once knew and lost and keep on seeking down in that well of loneliness.

But I never know what it was that I lost.

So I never find it, never.

*I hear you and I'm here for you. I hear the frustration and the pain. But aren't you leaving your energy **in** your addiction? Aren't you denying the creative life inside you? What's left for **you** and for loving?*

Good questions.

Let's keep talking and asking the questions. Maybe we'll stumble across some answers on the way!

My youngest son confronted me today in therapy. He's wondering about his sexual orientation and he asked me to come along to a session.

He said I had seduced him when he was a child. Me, his mother!

Of course I denied it. Flatly. I even got angry, and the therapist asked me what I was afraid of.

Afraid? I was mad.

Damned mad. And I still am.

Anyway, John says I used to dry him after his bath (I did, mothers do that), and sit him on my knee (of course I did), and then rub him in a sexual way (I didn't, I didn't).

John looked so sad today, so hurt.

Maybe I'll go to the next session and talk some more.

I think I should, don't you?

Yes I do. John needs to know that he's not crazy and making things up. You did play with him and masturbate him, we both know that. You can help John, and yourself, by getting things out in the open. Then we can get some help, too.

45

February 15
Filler

I used to create fantasies as a bridge between one affair and the next. When one man moved on, I'd have to have a stop-gap until the next came along.

I had to fill that gap.

I hated it when the whole day stretched out bleak and empty.

I hated it when there were no little luxuries on the horizon.

I hated it when I had a whole day without pleasure.

So I had this sheaf of fantasies, like a pack of cards, and I'd riffle through them and then settle down to a good old high.

I'd masturbate, of course, and sometimes even give myself a little pain.

Anything to stop just sitting around staring at reality.

> *You're pretty worthless, anyway. And so is reality. So if you didn't have your fantasies, you'd have nothing.*

Help me. Please help.

> *You're on your own, kid.*

You seem nervous and anxious this evening. Want to act out?

Yes. But I'm not going to.

> *How come? You need to get rid of some of that tension,
> you know.*

You're right. But I'm going to phone Jim and go for a walk around the lake.

> *Jim? But he's so boring—always going on and on
> about that Twelve Step group he's in.*

But that's exactly what I want to hear today.

> *Well, have it your way. Personally, I don't think any
> program can do you any good. You're a born
> exhibitionist, and even if you stop exposing yourself,
> you'll just do something else equally perverted.*

You make me laugh, sometimes. I can see you're just trying to get me mad so that I'll haul off and act out. But it doesn't work anymore, does it?

> *Well, no, I guess not.*

Let's work together on living a good, healthy life. It'll be better for both of us, you know.

> *Thanks for not getting mad and striking back. You're so
> different these days—it's going to take a while for me to
> get used to dealing with an adult and not a wayward
> child!*

February 17
Something special

This is hard to say, but I've often wanted to have sex play with children. Not violently, but just in a slow and dreamy kind of way.

I don't understand it, but it seems deeply sensuous to get close to kids again. Like going home. And then I suppose there's the power, the control.

This kept on happening, until one day I saw the fear in the child's eyes, and I knew I had to stop.

I never really did anything, you know, anything really wrong. But I came close to it more than once.

It's only since I've been in group that I can talk about this. I find understanding and support there, and the clasp of affection.

I'm beginning to find the trust and hope I never had as a child.

This used to split us apart, and I was the raging policeman, giving you hell for even thinking those thoughts. It's better now because of the group. You're beginning to feel that you are worth helping and healing. And I'm starting to feel that way about myself, too.

I start on the road to recovery and then I just give up.

It's not worth it, and anyway I'm not an addict, I just like a lot of sex, and it doesn't do any harm to anyone else, does it?

I feel so stupid and weak when I listen to all the other people in my group. But actually some of them are really prudish about sex. They're probably all repressed or afraid of doing it.

I like men, I like sex, I love it when they tell me I'm a real woman.

I do feel shame and disgust, it's true, but only sometimes.

Sometimes I do like having sex, if I know someone really well.

To tell the truth, I never get to know anyone well, as a matter of fact, and I never enjoy sex. I never feel safe, I'm never really there.

But what the hell—it's fun, isn't it? Isn't it?

> *You sound confused and scared. I used to encourage the chaos inside us—it gave me power. I want to change, and I hear from your pain that you want to change, too. Can we work together?*

I don't know. We can try, I guess. It's no fun alone.

February 19
Lonely

I used sex to break out of my isolation and I ended up feeling more lonely than ever.

What did you expect—applause?

How I hate that sneering voice of yours!

We all get what we deserve.

And what do you deserve?

Not much. But at least I'm not an addict.

You're part of me, so you're part of the disease. I'm working my way to sanity; why not join me?

Because we were born divided.

What a gloomy old fellow you are!

I'm the realist in the family. I know we'll never change.

We can change if we want to. Do you want to?

I'm fine as I am and where I am. Alone.

Many sex addicts say they are sociable, even gregarious, but often that means we sleep around a lot.

We put up walls to keep people out, and then we try to smash them down through random sex. And we think that's being sociable!

I acted like that all through my childhood, because I was afraid to let anyone know me. After all, I couldn't see how anyone could care for me when I didn't care for myself.

Recovery means that the walls come tumbling down. Then there's room to move and love and find our true being.

> *You loved to hide behind those walls, and you fooled a lot of people who admired you . . . from a distance. But I could always get at you, and I loved to be your harshest critic. And now? The old games just don't work anymore.*

No. And now our voices are beginning to work in harmony again.

> *New life, new voices.*

February 21
Having and being

When I was a kid I didn't know if I wanted to be like people I admired or possess them.

> *Well, what did you decide?*

I didn't. That was the trouble.

> *Did it have to be one or the other?*

How do you mean?

> *Couldn't you just be yourself?*

No, that was the problem. I didn't know who I was, apart from other people. And now, when I love someone, I don't know where I am.

> *Maybe you should spend some time being out of love for a change.*

Why?

> *To establish some boundaries and come home.*

Home?

> *Yes, home to you.*

Sounds like a good idea. I'll give it a try.

I used to think I was just highly sexed and interested in exploring my sexuality. I couldn't understand why I never felt really good about it afterwards.

I'd say to myself, "It's okay, I needn't feel bad, after all, everyone likes sex, don't they?"

I'd think, "I'll just see him once more, then I'll move on"; or "I really do need sex, and anyway it doesn't do anyone any harm"; and "Well, after all, I like sex, and my life's my own."

Looking back, I can see how many little clues and little lies were there in all those voices. I wasn't just highly sexed, I was a sex addict feeling lonely and let down, making excuses.

I don't want to go on living like that, still hearing those voices right up until I die.

That's why I'm glad to be a member of a group where all those little lies just don't work.

> *I can see now that it must have been hard living those lies. At the time, of course, I loved it, because the more little lies you told, the more I made you squirm. That little game doesn't work anymore now, does it?*

No. We both see through it, don't we?

February 23
Trespass

You remember when I was a kid, Dad was always touching me and giving me little tickles and squeezes?

> *Well, what of it?*

I've been talking about it in my group and starting to remember things I'd blanked out for years.

> *Listen, you don't need to worry about the old days. They're dead and gone.*

Exactly. I've been missing my childhood—not that I want to live the way I did, but that I've lost it.

> *Lost it? How do you mean?*

I blotted it out. It was Dad, Dad. He molested me, that's the truth of it.

> *How can you even think that?*

Because it's true . . . and now I can talk about it and finally begin to find out who I am and set up my own boundaries.

> *Well, that's a switch. It was always "Daddy said and Daddy thinks and Daddy knows." Are you sure you know what you're talking about? Maybe we could talk more about this without fighting. What do you think?*

I think we can. I know we can.

When I was a kid, my dad beat me a lot with his belt.

I was pretty high-spirited and often in some minor scrape; and the punishment was always the same—the belt.

Worse than the pain was the humiliation. I crawled off into my room and hunted around for something to take the pain and the shame away. And then, of course, I discovered masturbation—the perfect antidote to shame and pain . . . or so I thought.

I said to myself I didn't care, and in some ways I didn't—as long as I had **that**. But then it became a habit, and whenever I felt emotional or physical pain, I'd turn to **that**. And **that** became my refuge, my obsession, my compulsion, my life.

> Yes, it really crept up on you until it took you over. But now you can talk about it, and that's part of the First Step on the path to recovery.

And then?

> And then, the Second Step!

February 25
Dancing

You'll never make it, never in a thousand years.

What a Big Voice you have, granny wolf.

> *You love that sex, that addictive, selfish, self-hating sex,
> and you'll never give it up.*

What a Big Mouth you have, granny wolf.

> *You're an addict, an addict, an addict.*

What little teeth you have, after all, granny wolf! And I used
to be so scared of you, scared of you and your voice and your
teeth—and that would make me want to run to my addiction.
But now I'm healing. I don't need to listen to you anymore
when you're playing the Big Bad Wolf. Aren't you getting
tired of it?

> *I suppose I am. It's beginning to sound like a boring
> old record, and I don't want to make you dance
> anymore.*

You **can't** make me dance anymore, can you?

> *No.*

Don't sound so sad, granny. We can try being friends.

> *Can we really? That would be great.*

Come on, old dear. Let's dance!

> *Well, all that new energy and life! You'll wear me out,
> young man.*

Dance, my dear, dance!

I can't get along with myself. I can't see myself or feel myself as real. I can only hide in my shame.

> *Yes, but you can't hide from me. I can see into your shame. I know you inside out and I know every single one of your squalid little secrets.*

Why are you always so harsh and sadistic? Your voice isn't mine, it comes from outside, from school, from my step-father, from beyond.

> *No, it's part of you now, and you'll never get rid of it as long as you stay locked in your shame and your isolation.*

You're blind. You're wrong, dead wrong. I'm not alone anymore, thanks to my friends in the Program. I'm on my way out of shame, and soon you'll have nothing to yell about, you'll see.

> *Well, it's true that I often can't get to you the way I used to. You're feeling better and it's beginning to show. What's going on?*

I'm out of my shame. Want to join me?

> *Is there a place for me?*

Yes. A place in the sun. I'll get you a rocking chair, old fellow!

February 27
Denying the obvious

Even after I knew in my gut that I was a sex addict, I went on denying it in my head.

"I'm just on edge these days," or "I have a strong libido," or "I don't handle stress that well"—these are the kinds of phrases that ran though my mind and blocked out the voices that were telling me I needed help.

Finally, one evening I was tempted to slip into the bedroom of one of my daughter's friends—not just because I was "edgy," but because I felt attracted to her. I was out of control.

And that's when I knew I needed help.

In therapy I still went on denying that I was addicted until one day a friend suggested I join a Twelve Step group. When I heard other people's stories, I immediately identified with them, and last week I spoke up and admitted my powerlessness.

Powerlessness over my sex addiction.

Yes, that's the first step. I'm really proud that you said it and that you mean to do something about it. And don't forget—I'm on your side.

What do you want to go downtown for?

Just to check out the stores.

>*Bookstores?*

I need some new computer stuff.

>*Stuff?*

Yes. Programs. You know.

>*Graphics programs?*

What's this? The Watergate hearings?

>*You said it! Same kind of sleaze.*

Sleaze?

>*Yes. You know how Jock described those graphics
>programs . . . graphically. There's computer
>pornography, just like any other kind of pornography.
>And you know it, don't you?*

Yes. Of course there is. But that doesn't mean that I . . .

>*Time out! Look, I'm here, with you all the time, and all
>the way, if you want. You can't deceive me anymore
>than you can deceive yourself. So let's just be straight
>with each other and take it from here, as adults.*

Adults, as in Adult Bookstores?

>*Adults, as in real life!*

59

February 29
The moment

Once I was sitting in a Greek restaurant watching two lovers at a nearby table. I say they were lovers because, although they were middle-aged, they were obviously in love.

But they weren't so in love with each other or themselves that they forgot to be in love with life. Everything that happened around them, inside the cafe and in the little harbor just across the road, seemed to fascinate and provoke them. They sat there for hours, and I never heard either of them emoting about the past or plunging into self-analysis.

They sat there together, companionably, attentive to each other and to life as it moved and created its being around them—the passers-by, the fishermen in their blue and golden boats dancing on the waves, the nets stretched out on the quay, the food piled up on the plates, the lovely rough local wine, the priest drowsing in the sun outside, even the flies on the checkered tablecloth.

When they left to walk home, I smiled and said, "Thank you."

Yes, I can still see that day. How real it was, each moment. It's so good to remember and savor the little things—they keep us sane and attached to life.

60

My husband always had pornography in the house and he'd spend time alone with it, almost from the day we got married.

Sometimes he brought home lingerie and asked me to put it on before we made love. Later he told me that he wanted me to look like one of the women in his magazine.

I was angry, but I was also curious. So I started paging through the piles of pornography he kept in a closet in the basement. To my surprise I started getting excited looking at some of the pictures.

Then for about a year I became addicted to gazing at the magazines. I found that I was drawn to the situations and positions where the woman is the victim.

It was when I felt like asking my husband to beat me that I knew I needed help.

I've been in a Twelve Step group for three years now, and last year my husband also joined a group.

We threw the magazines into the garbage, together.

We're going to make it.

Yes. I know, and I'm really glad. I give you all the credit; I was too busy beating on you and keeping you in shame. Recovery has been like a breath of fresh air through the whole system!

March 2
Star

At school everything was going for me . . . magna cum laude, sports, girls, cars, Florida, Aspen.

Straight into Dad's business, too good to be true. Me and my old man, buddies, just buddies out for a good time and a lot of money, I mean a lot of money to go round.

Poor old Mom stuck at home night after night. On the town, Dad and me, two old buddies.

He'd find me the girls. He had this knack. "And this is my boy, Charlie, the best son a man could have . . . and a great body." Whisper, nudge, wink, leer.

I'd take them home and screw them for him. For him. He heard everything. I saw it in his eyes the next day.

He's dead now.

I'm still carrying on.

For him.

Here, just a minute. This is crazy, you're you, not your old man. And I'm not your old man. Your old man's dead, and you're alive. Hold on, don't run, hold it right there. We need help. We'll get it, together.

I never knew how Dad was going to react. He was always working, always tired, always angry.

He was unpredictable, too. I'd be late for a meal and he'd blow up. I'd be late a few days later and he'd give me a smile.

I'd get nervous and spill my milk. He'd hit me and send me up to my room. An hour later he'd want to play basketball with me out in the yard.

I could never really talk to him about me. There were things I wanted to get straight—about sex and stuff. I couldn't get through to him.

He kept telling me to be a man. What was that—angry, tired, selfish, unpredictable?

So I gave up and withdrew.

I gave up on life.

And became an addict.

———————————

You sound hopeless to me. I get tired, too, tired of your whining and your self-indulgence. Dad was trying to make a man of you. Why can't you do what he said—be a man?

March 4
Nothing to hide

In my humiliation I seek another's mortification, like seeking like.

> *Can you explain that?*

I show myself, not because I have something to show but because I have nothing to show for it.

> *In your acting out, you mean.*

Showing off, acting out, exhibiting myself. Perverted math: "I've got nothing to hide," equals "I've got one," equals "I've got nothing."

> *And straddling that crazy math, more humiliation?*

Yes. First my mother's. Humiliating me for her own wound. Then I pass it on, out of fear and desperation.

> *How it runs and bleeds, that wound!*

Runs and bleeds from generation to generation and humiliation to humiliation.

> *Until, one day, it gets understood, loved, and healed.*

By whom?

> *By us—the victim and the executioner. Yes, we can do it.*

How?

> *Talking, joining a group, working.*

I'm with you.

 My mother used to flirt with me when I was a young boy. I would come into her room and find her just slipping something on, teasingly.

And then she would come and watch me take a bath and caress me with her eyes.

As I grew up, I avoided her seductive ways—and yet I missed them. Messages about sex became confused and scary. I found I wanted to be looked at and admired, and yet I fled from intimacy.

I got my balance back in a Twelve Step program. Talking openly, admitting my insecurities, listening to others—all helped me free myself from the tangle of contradictory messages.

Now I want to be able to create love instead of just submitting to seductiveness.

———————————

You sound healthy to me. I nearly said, "and it's about time," as I always did in the old days. But I'm learning to be positive; our relationship deserves it.

March 6
Responsibility

It's not fair, you know.

>*What isn't fair?*

My addiction. It's not my fault. Sex was something forced on me too early as a kid. I was abused by my cousin, you know that?

>*Yes, I do. You were the sweet little girl, and then the victim.*

Don't laugh. It still hurts.

>*Sorry.*

And, if I was a victim, I can't help it, can I, if I just go on repeating that pattern?

>*It's hard, I know. But don't you think you have the responsibility to recover? That's what the Program is all about.*

Yes, I do see that. But what if I can't go it alone?

>*But you're not alone. You have support now, and a new source of power.*

I see what you mean. It's up to me to get well, and now there's a context, a community. And then there's you. How are you going to be?

>*We'll see. I'm changing, too, you know. And we know it helps that you and I can take our different responsibilities and work together. Working together, you and I, now that's something new!*

Why do you always treat me like an object?

> *Because that's how you treat other people. You don't care about them as human beings. You just want them for your pleasure.*

That's not true. I know I used to be like that, but I'm changing, you know.

> *Are you? Once an addict, always an addict, that's what they say!*

You sound pleased to keep putting me down. But I'm stronger now, and I can see an end to this addiction. I'm learning to appreciate other people for who they are and not just what I can get out of them.

> *Good. When you really do treat people as people, you'll see a change in my attitude to you. I think we can strike a bargain, don't you?*

Yes I do. And it feels good to hear your voice talking kindly to me rather than shouting and criticizing all the time.

> *Yes, okay, I'm with you. I guess we must have learned to treat people like objects somewhere. And what we learned, we can always unlearn, don't you agree?*

Yes. But it's hard.

> *That's life.*

Still preaching a bit, old Supervoice!

March 8
Passion

I used to think I was passionate, but really I was addicted. Addicted to fantasy, to images, to acting out.

I liked to think of myself as the Great Seducer, but all I wanted was to be adored. And when my partner asked for affection and tenderness, I thought he was silly and weak.

A quiet voice inside me kept telling me that I was in need of help, but I drowned it out with the shrill voice of passion and egoism.

Now I hear that quiet voice loud and clear.

That's what recovery is all about: listening to the voice of real needs and getting help and sharing affection.

———————————

Yes, you did yell and scream and think you were God's gift to men. Now you can see that God's gift is having a loving heart.

Whenever I see capital letters on a printed page, I THINK IT'S MY DAD SPEAKING.

>   *What do you mean?*

When he was mad, which was often, he spoke quietly but with that cruel and cutting emphasis you see in capital letters.

>   *Yes, I think I see what you're getting at.*

You should—because sometimes you take over his voice, and I'm seeing those capital letters again.

>   ***WHAT DO YOU MEAN?***

That's exactly what I mean. Just look at you, there, on the page!

>   *Mm. I see. It does look a bit intimidating.*

It's not a bit intimidating. IT'S DOWNRIGHT SCARY.

>   *All right, all right. No need to shout.*

Get it?

>   *Yes. Thanks. That's something I need to work on.*

March 10
Change

You've been rather silent of late, my Supervoice!

> *Quiet, child.*

Listen. I'm an adult and I love it. Is that the trouble?

> *Well, if you really want to know.*

I do, yes. Go on.

> *I feel I'm losing you. There's no connection anymore.*
> *We used to be so comfortable in our roles.*

Father and son? Judge and criminal? Executioner and victim?

> *Was it really like that?*

It felt like that to me. How about you?

> *It was awful.*

We can change. We are changing. It's painful to reorient the various elements in a personality, but that's what's happening, and that's what I want and need.

> *Do I want that? Or am I happy in my old role?*

You tell me.

> *Tomorrow.*

Now.

> *I want to change, too.*

I always knew there was something in the family history—a trace, a shadow, a secret.

I thought maybe my mother was a lesbian—she seemed so close to her sister, and they often seemed to be fascinated and yet somehow disgusted by sex.

I knew there was something there, but I couldn't get to it.

At times, when I masturbated, I thought I might find the answer—but of course I never did.

Yesterday, after therapy, I sat down with my mother, and for once we had an honest, open talk. She told me she had been molested by her father for five years when she was a teenager. And for years she had just clamped it all down and kept it as a secret.

And the secret was there in the family all the time, affecting all of us, all those years.

Like a shadow.

———————————

That does explain a lot, doesn't it? And now we can get to work with this new knowledge, even though it's scary. Let's start right now.

March 12
Anonymous

Who am I? I don't know myself; I'm lost in my addiction.

> *I'll tell you who you are: you're nobody, nothing, just a sex addict.*

Heaven help me! I need help. I need to come back to me.

> *There's no way back. You're doomed, damned, out of it.*

Look. I'm tired of your telling me that I'm nothing but an addict. I don't have to listen to that voice forever.

> *Well. . . . Go on.*

I'm finding my own voice, telling my own story, inventing my own life.

> *You see, it's just a fiction!*

No, it's my story, I'm creating my life, my own life, mine. And I want you to be on my side. Will you? I don't trust you, as things are: you're so unpredictable.

> *I don't trust myself yet either. My voice isn't my own yet; I'm still just an echo of Mom and Dad.*

Let's work on it. We can change.

> *Together?*

Together.

Y̲ou know, I never knew what I was looking for when I dated all those men in college. One after the other, plenty of sex, but no meaning.

> *Trying to fill the void?*

Yes, I suppose that was it. I wanted to remain faithful, but to whom?

> *Dad?*

Yes, maybe. I loved him so much, and it was an impossible kind of love. I couldn't make him feel or hear all I wanted him to know.

> *He knew.*

Do you think so? Oh, that makes me feel good! I thought I had to keep proving my loyalty to him over and over again.

> *By being unfaithful to your lovers?*

Sounds weird, but maybe that was it. Maybe the person I really need to be faithful to is . . .

> *You?*

Yes, that's it. Me.

> *It's really good to talk like this. It's a way of getting our story straight and out in the open. What a difference it makes!*

March 14
Fragile

I like groups usually. I mean, I've been in sales most of my life and I'm into people. In fact, my friends say I'm the most people-oriented guy they know. And a first-rate salesman.

I can run a meeting, give a sales pitch, and put just about anything over. And I like the feedback and the kudos, after a good talk or a great sale.

I come across powerfully. I took this course on projection, and the teacher said I was one of the stars.

I like being a star. I like the feedback, like I said, and the look in people's eyes when I'm talking.

It's the same with women. They love to watch my act and hear me talk and then, whoops, off to bed.

It's one big laugh.

You talk like this to drown me out. You know you're scared and lonely and the rest is just baloney and bluster. There's one group I think you really need to join, a Twelve Step group on sex addiction. You'd be a star there, all right!

Talking is like exercise.

> *Go on.*

I mean, for so long my head was just full of all these voices, shouting, cursing, fighting, blaming—never listening, never learning. Always the same old tapes.

> *And now?*

Now we're trying on new voices, struggling to get somewhere together. Practicing new voices. Making ourselves anew. I need that.

> *Yes, you do . . . and, well, so do I.*

I'm glad you said that. For so long you were just the same old tape, repeating those tired old messages of failure and punishment.

> *Yes, I know. Those were the bad old tapes for both of us. I'm glad we're listening to each other now. It sure makes a difference.*

Thanks. I agree. Let's keep on with this; it's good to hear.

> *You know, I didn't realize how tired I was of being judge, jury, and executioner. I'm glad you're speaking in a new voice.*

We both need practice. You too, you know.

> *Of course. Practice makes perfect, dear child.*

Practice makes us human, old man.

March 16
Pedestal

My first girlfriend was pure as the driven snow. Her hair was sunny like spun gold, her eyes sea-blue, and her soul was as golden as her hair.

> *Was she real? Sounds rather bookish to me.*

You're right. Straight from a book, a medieval tale of chivalry that I found in the school library. It had a picture of this goddess on the cover and I was hoping for some sex.

> *Under the covers?*

That's the way it was. A princess in the house across the street and solitary sex beneath the bedclothes.

> *Were you in love?*

In love with the princess, in lust with myself. That's the way it often is for men, you know.

> *We're talking about you. Trying to heal.*

Heal?

> *The split. Heal the split in you, the split that keeps you in your addiction and us apart.*

I see. I don't mean to be flippant. Let's keep talking about this.

> *Yes. And let's start by dismantling those pedestals.*

I used to have a diary in which I kept all my secret thoughts. Some of them were trivial, some were silly, some were private and secret. All of them were mine.

Mom read it when I was away at camp. "Darling, is this really how you feel about yourself?" "I'm shocked at all that dirty sex talk." "I just can't believe you do **that**."

Everyone knows what **that** is. It's always **that** or **it**. People say, "When she's by herself, she does **that**." Or, a guy says, "Why don't we go to my place and do **it**?"

I just looked at Mom. Then I went upstairs and got my diary, ripped out the pages, and threw them on the living-room fire.

Mom just stood there. Smug.

I went back to my room, locked the door, and did **that**. When I came, I cried.

Now I do **that** a lot.

And I still cry.

---

*I can't believe you still do **that**, at your age! You didn't learn anything from Mom, did you? You blame her for everything, but don't forget you started it. And she tried to love you, even so. She still does love you, and always will. Always.*

March 18
Spring

Where did I get all this energy?

> *Well, it's spring, isn't it?*

Yes. But it's been spring before, but I've never felt like this.

> *What else is going on?*

I've stopped going to pornographic bookstores and having sex with men in the booths.

> *Might that be it?*

The new energy? Because I'm not masturbating? Surely you don't believe in that old stuff.

> *No, not the physical side, the mental side—the fact that you're not thinking of sex all the time, morning, noon, and night. Not fantasizing. Not leering at those videos. Not imagining the perfect partner, the ideal high, the sexual paradise that always turns out to be a desert of shame.*

Well, come to think of it . . .

> *Yes. I'm glad you're thinking about your new energy instead of about sex all the time—that anonymous sex that always promises the sky and ends up in sackcloth and ashes. Let's harness all that new energy to change!*

I sat under the piano and watched my cousin play. I listened to him playing Chopin and tears came into my eyes. I must have been three. I loved him.

Later I thought about him all the time, wanting him to come back.

My parents sent me away to school, a military kind of school, with cold showers before breakfast and everything controlled and righteous. They knew and didn't want to know.

The boys all laughed at queers and faggots. I trembled in the shower and laughed at the jokes that went right through my skin like arrows.

I liked art and gazed at Greek statues, young boys at play. And I drove my secret down, down, down, out of sight and out of mind.

I've never loved anyone or anything . . . except pictures.

How harsh it all was, and demeaning. But now, in the group, we hear men owning their feelings and sexual orientations. There's strength there and courage to be yourself at last. Let's tear up that pornography and live!

March 20
Astray

Do you think that we are born innocent and pure?

Yes and no.

Don't play the sphinx, my friend.

I think we're born innocent—of personal sin, or vice. But we do have the potential to go astray, and as little kids we can be mean and selfish and nasty and brutal.

And addicted?

What do you think?

I believe addiction is a deviation, a displacement. Sexual energy is turned away and displaced onto something else.

Isn't sex always to some extent a displacement?

You mean a displacement from the Absolute of Desire to the here and now, the this and the that, a touch, a kiss, a promise?

So why isn't sex always an addiction?

Because the energy can be directed and apportioned, and we can learn to encompass it with affection.

So what is sex addiction?

Sex without boundaries or proportion or balance or affection.

*Now **you** are providing the answers. That's great!*

But don't I sound just a touch pompous, like . . .

Like me, you mean?

You said it, old boy!

It's strange. I prefer to love from a distance and build up images in my mind.

I love movies and TV, but I always sit far away and half-close my eyes.

Then between me and the screen there's a zone of make-believe. I feel free there, creative even.

My mother undressed once in my room when Dad was gone. I loved the slowness of it and the fragrance of her hair.

Close-up of her nakedness, stark and near! I closed my eyes in terror.

I feel that terror now.

> *I laughed at that terror once, and I feel you've never forgiven me. I know it's real. I'm sorry.*

It's not enough to be sorry.

> *No, we have to change.*

I can't change.

March 22
Winning

A friend at my group told me that the tension reaches a peak for about ten seconds and then subsides. "Just ride it out," he said. "You can win."

Sounds like good advice to me. Let's try it.

I tried it yesterday. I lost. And then I acted out.

And did that help with the tension?

Yes. Right away. For a while. But then I felt tense again and added to the tension was the anger and the shame.

So you lost twice over.

I suppose you could say that. But anyway, I thought we weren't going to think of life in terms of winning and losing.

Very clever! But that had to do with competing with other people. We don't need that, no.

But not acting out is competing with yourself, isn't it?

No. It's recognizing that you prefer to belong to a nonaddictive system rather than an addictive system.

I see. Thanks. I like the way we talk, these days.

Me too. I think we need to go on with this conversation. The Program is a new set of relationships, not a competition.

Let me do it, I want it so badly.

> *Sure, that's okay. Go ahead.*

You won't get mad and beat me up?

> *Of course I will, but do it anyway. You enjoy yourself.*

I don't trust that voice of yours. You're setting me up.

> *Look, you're worthless anyway, so what does it matter? Have some fun.*

It isn't fun anymore. You know that. And I have choices, don't I?

> *You think you do. But really, you always end up in the same place.*

You know what? I don't have to listen to you; you're not the boss anymore. I've found out some things about myself that I really like—and one of them is trusting my own judgment. From now on, I'm the one who's going to make the decisions. I mean it—and it feels great to trust my own word.

> *I thought I could still rule you and mess you about. I'm losing my power. It's that group of yours, isn't it?*

Yes. And my hard work. Don't forget that.

> *Credit where credit is due?*

That's right. Want to join me?

March 24
Phantom

If there's an odd number of steps here, going up to class . . . he'll come for me, tonight. Twenty-three! He'll be there.

Or at least I'll get a call—collect, probably, but I'll pay.

"Anna loves you, always," I'll say it, whatever he says. It's true. Anna's here for you now, this second, and always will be.

He needs to go off, men do, they just have to go sometimes. He told me so, and I believe him. "Anna, it's stronger than me, I have to go."

He'll come for our baby . . . he wanted it so badly, too. And even if he didn't, I'll want it for both of us. And want him back, always.

I know he'll come. There's this bond, this love.

Oh love!

Can I say something? I mean, he's been gone three months and not a word, not a call. Can you accept what's happened? Let me help. You're still here and alive. Let's talk, walk, move on.

For a long time I thought that I was rotten to the core—a bad apple, rotting on the ground after the harvest.

That's certainly true.

I didn't want to let anyone close to me, because I knew that it would only be a matter of time before they stripped away the outer layers and found the core of rottenness and filth inside.

More than filth—degradation and decay.

Yes, degradation. Perversion and obscenity.

Filth. Garbage. Subhuman.

Yes, you're right. Subhuman filth and garbage.

And you'll never get out, never make it.

Never get out. Never make it.

Lost. Damned.

Damned.

Good boy. That's what I like to hear.

March 26
Unknown

I feel scared most of the time. Even when I'm happy there's a current of fear.

When I act out, I'm scared. When I'm sober I'm frightened that it won't last.

I'm not a coward. I saw a child drowning once, at the lake. I ran along the dock and jumped in even though I wasn't a good swimmer. And I don't mind walking home alone after work in the winter when it's dark.

It's not that. I'm scared because I think something's going to happen, something I can't control. Like falling in love and being swept away.

That's why the sex I like best is with myself.

But even then, I'm scared.

> *Remember last time at the group? John said the more he tried to control things, the more he felt scared. And you agreed.*

Yes. That's true.

> *Let's talk more about that. I think there's a clue there we can follow up. Unless, of course, you like being in control . . . and scared.*

I've always had enough money to get by.

> *And yet we lived all those years in poverty.*

We had a lot of fun, you know. I hate it when you say our life was the pits.

> *We thought we were having fun, but there was no shared pleasure, not even between you and me.*

What do you mean?

> *You were scared of me and I was busy making you feel guilty for acting out.*

Yes. And then the shame.

> *And the anger.*

I deserved it.

> *Not all of it.*

I did, really.

> *Don't keep contradicting me!*

Oops. I see what you mean. How funny it sounds, that old tape!

> *Yes. It's so easy to slip back into the old positions and the old voices. But now there's a difference. We can laugh our way out again.*

March 28
Picture postcards

I read in a book recently that sex addicts often can't talk about their childhoods, so instead they send picture postcards.

"Having a wonderful childhood. Wish you were here."

"Everything in my childhood garden is rosy this year."

Parents love these postcards. They sit and read them and smile cozily—especially parents who neglected or abused their children. It's weird how those cards make them feel so cozy. And it's even weirder that their children keep sending them. "Wish you were here—the way I always wanted."

Often there's a hidden message—a cry of pain, or a guarded insult, but the parents don't see it. All they see is what they want to see: the sun on the grass and the flowers in bloom in that cozy, magical garden.

I've sent hundreds of these postcards, hundreds and hundreds.

But not anymore.

---

*I'm glad—glad for both of us. We've stopped telling lies and collaborating with our parents' smug and lying version of history. Now we can create our past and our own life and call it **our own**.*

I'm beginning to feel better about myself.

> *Really? You seem just the same to me.*

How do you mean?

> *You're still lazy, selfish, untrustworthy, dirty, and weak.*

That sounds like my parents speaking. You've taken over their bullying tone.

> *Well, you're still a child and always will be.*

No, you're wrong, I'm my own person now, and I've found a warm and friendly new family in my group.

> *That won't last, you'll see.*

Yes, we'll see. I'm just not going to listen to your icy words anymore. Maybe one day we can talk like human beings, but for now I'm finding my own voice at last.

> *I can see this is going to be a struggle. We'll see who wins. I've got a lot of ammunition on my side, you know. Addict!*

March 30
Odd spots

Wwhat gets me about sex addiction is the weird places you end up in the morning.

> *Like where?*

You know . . . . That time I woke up in a guy's closet because his mom came home early . . . another time in a laundromat . . . in Barbados in a swamp . . . and then in cars, boats, trailers, even a coal cellar, you name it.

> *Was it fun?*

No, it was crazy, you know that. I mean, who wants to wake up in a heap of dirty clothes—just for a one-night stand with a guy who happens to own a laundromat.

> *I get the point.*

Do you? I'm glad. For so long you'd be the first to say "I told you so," or "Serves you right," or "Good riddance to bad rubbish." Sounds as though you're changing, too.

> *Yes, I know. I was a brute. And I sure as heck didn't have fun in that laundromat or that swamp, either. I'm sorry—for both of us. We'll do better.*

I got tired of hearing inner voices saying that I was weak and worthless and shameful and hateful.

They came from far away, those voices, but they sounded close inside my head, like sirens. Sometimes I used to feel they were driving me crazy.

I don't know exactly where they came from or when they started; but now that doesn't interest me, because they're slowly dying away.

I've found other voices to put in their places, voices that are helpful and kindly.

These new voices speak to me like friends, like brothers, like true lovers.

And they are mine.

Yes, yes, yes. How great it is to hear you say that! And it feels good to be close to you and on your side.

April 1
Fulfilled

I've got to have it now or I'll go crazy.

If she doesn't love me I'll die.

I need a car; I deserve it; it makes me mad to think that everyone can have one except me.

Mom let me eat what I wanted and when I wanted. She encouraged me to be free. This is a free society, isn't it? Why shouldn't I have what I want? And have it now!

Women want to be loved, held, spoiled. I make myself available and give them what they want.

I'm bored if I'm not dating.

I'm bored with the person I'm dating.

I've got to move. Move on.

Demand and supply, that's the law of our society. I wouldn't live anywhere else. It's a great place to hustle.

How come I always feel lonely?

———————

Well, to be old-fashioned about it, you're lonely because you're self-indulgent, self-centered, and self-concerned. You're just a selfish little consumer, addicted to yourself and to sex. That's what you want and that's what you've got. There's no hope. None.

My therapist suggested that I join a Twelve Step group for sex addiction. I joined the Program three months ago.

I listen to the guys talking there and frankly I'm amazed. Some of them can't think or talk about anything else but sex. They seem to be doing it all the time, with one woman after another. And the gays and the fetishists and the cross-dressers and the window peepers and the flashers—man, it's a crazy world. Makes the *National Enquirer* look like a kid's comic.

I can't seem to relate to that kind of stuff. I'm real private about sex, myself. And I've never done anyone any harm. In fact I've never done anything sexual with anyone. And I don't peep or flash or cruise.

I just sit at home with my pictures and videos and get high. It's true I masturbate, three or four times a day—more sometimes.

None of that crazy stuff for me.

————————

*Could you stop, though? What about your
work—you're always late, you know, and below par.
You get angry easily, too. And you spend more and
more time with your pornography. Aren't these signs
that you're not managing your life? Let's stick with the
Program, for a while. I think it can energize us and
help us break free.*

April 3
Self-love

People tell me it would be good if I learned to love myself, but then others say self-love is selfish and narcissistic.

In my addiction I often gazed at myself like Narcissus, falling in love with his own gorgeous reflection, in a mirror or a pool or a pornographic picture.

I see now that this attachment was an attempt to cover over feelings of inadequacy and shame. I wanted to "fall in love" with an ideal image of myself to mask the pain of being me.

Why not be me? What's wrong with that? Can't I learn to live with me and to like myself?

Liking myself can lead to affection and then love—the clear-sighted love for a real live human being, frailties and all.

———————

*Good for you. Good for us. I think we're getting there,
making good distinctions, growing, coming home.
What you are is fine with me.*

We've been having a good time lately, you and I.

> *That's easy for you to say.*

Why? What's wrong?

> *You.*

What is it now?

> *You're just the same—lazy, feckless, selfish.*

That's your opinion.

> *Go on. Run. Act out. Sex fiend.*

No thanks. I feel strong and healthy. Why don't you join me?

> *You the strong one! That's a switch. Well, come to think
> of it, I do feel you getting stronger.*

I am getting stronger. How about you?

> *Yes. Me, too. I have to admit it.*

Is it hard to admit it?

> *Yes. But I can admit it, thanks in part to you.*

April 5
Programming

I like my computer, partly because I can't figure it all out.

It's got a friendly face, and even smiles at me when I turn it on. Not that it's cute—I don't mean that. It doesn't say, "Hi, Pete, this is your friend. Have a good day."

It's not fake, in that way. It's reserved, discreet. It shows things on the screen and does the things I ask, most of the time. But behind the screen, it has its own agenda, its own program, written in code.

Even if I could see it, I couldn't understand it. It's just not my language, yet it's connected with what I do.

It's a special script, programmed to make things happen. Sometimes I can choose, sometimes it makes the decisions.

It's like my unconscious. I used to be scared of not always being in control of it; but I don't feel like that anymore.

Sometimes it's great just to let things happen.

Yes, I agree! Always trying to be in control drives us crazy—and others, too. It's often healthy to let that "other language" take over for a while.

My parents let me stay in their bed when they made love. I can't remember much except the noise.

You don't want to remember, do you?

I said, I can't remember.

Try.

I was too young.

And too scared. You're still scared.

You like that, don't you? You love my fear, just like Dad. I think he wanted me there in bed to show me who was boss.

He was the boss.

You live off my fear like a parasite. That makes me think you're the one who's afraid.

Afraid of what, may I ask?

My health, my sanity, my independence.

April 7
Old pro

"Excuse me, don't I know you, weren't you in my class on Swinburne?" She laughs, there's that smile in my voice. Lithe and young, high cheekbones. Sharp.

Now! There's the glance, the signal. "Well, I should know you, my dear, I'd like to, I mean. How about coffee?" The thread tightens . . . and holds.

Plunge into the unknown, brazen glance and gesture. Smooth, with a hint of wildness, a slight rasp to the voice. Words over coffee. Literature, of course.

"Tonight, after dinner, the library, third floor."

Pupils spin, focus. Hold there. Reel in. "English major? Meet you by the Romantics. Swinburne? We could read a little poetry and then . . . "

The poetry, the wine, the same old story.

She's grown up, a student.

I'm fun. I'm lonely.

It's just fun.

———————

Fun? You'll leave her and hurt her or hurt her and leave her, it makes no difference. She'll be hurt. And you? For you, there's nothing. Not any fun, even. Nothing.

Empathy is based on trust. I can empathize with another person because I am secure in myself.

In my addiction, I was full of anxiety and worried about being taken over by others if I got too close to them.

So I kept my distance and took refuge in the dark room of my addiction. I closed myself off from the world.

Now that I feel confident in myself and in my boundaries, I can reach out to others and feel for them as separate people, worthy of love and compassion.

It's good to have found fellow-feeling at last.

>*Yes, that's what empathy is—fellow-feeling. Can we get that going between us?*

Let's try. Of course you still love to play the teacher, dear Supervoice; but I think we can work on that, too, old fellow!

April 9
Business

Dad owned a bar in a large midwestern city. I grew up in an atmosphere of booze and sex, and my dad was proud of my looks and made me work behind the bar. It was good for business.

Men liked me. I was blonde and outspoken and old for my age. I always fell for the quiet guys who were having trouble at home. I slept around a lot, and then one day, a guy left a hundred dollars on the dressing table in my room.

I left home and hooked up with an escort service. The money was good and the clients classy. I said to myself it was only for a couple of years till I got on my feet.

It's been five years now, and I'm still on my back.

I want to get out.

I'm sick of using my body as a business.

It'll be hard. People like pointing a finger at prostitutes. It's organized sex addiction, but they don't see it that way. We need to get into one of those Twelve Step groups and take it from there. Come on. Let's do it!

*D*idn't it hurt when Gary called you a playboy the other day?

No. Why should it?

> *You're forty-five, and he was calling you a boy. Doesn't that worry you?*

He didn't say "boy," he said "playboy." That means I'm mellow; I get around.

> *But what do you get around to?*

Having fun. You know that.

> *Let me be honest. I just don't see how it can be fun for a middle-aged man to run around with college-age women and have three different sexual partners every week.*

I'm a busy man. I play the market during the day and the field at night. Works well for me.

> *You make it sound as if women are like stocks and shares—something to manipulate and profit from.*

You're right. I like to dabble.

> *I don't seem to be getting through to you today. Let's talk some more tomorrow. There's a men's group I think we should join.*

April 11
Getting mad

I've always thought it interesting that getting angry is known as getting mad, as if there were a connection between anger and madness.

I remember my dad in a rage, shouting, screaming, foaming at the mouth, out of control. That seemed like madness to me, and it made me sick and terrified to be alive.

Now they say I should get mad myself. I'm scared I'll sound like Dad. How ugly that would be.

And yet I have all this confusion inside myself—pain, fear, anger—and I know it feeds my addiction and drives me out of control.

So I'm trying to let my anger out when I feel angry. I think I've earned that right. But I have to be honest about what upsets me.

I just have to find out what I'm angry about in the here and now and focus my anger on that.

> *Yes. And I'll try not to be mad with you. I know that I sometimes used to rage and fume and kill all joy and peace for us. I didn't mean to; it seemed as if another voice took over. It sounded like Dad all over again. I'm glad we're getting together on this and working it out.*

Relationships, relationships, relationships, why doesn't anyone ever talk about being alone?

> *Because they're all scared, don't you think?*

Yes I do. In our culture everyone has to be in a sexual relationship, otherwise you're a loner, a failure.

> *And you?*

I feel strong, you know, and I'm learning to enjoy my own company. I joined a group and learned to enjoy being alone. What do you think of that?

> *That figures. The group gives us the strength to be ourselves, and then we have the power to be alone. We can learn a lot in solitude, it's a restful and creative place to be.*

That's right. It gives all our voices a chance to work things out and create something new.

> *It's good to hear you talking like that. It makes me realize how much I'm changing, too. From parent to friend—and I like it that way.*

April 13
Going on

I want to go back.

> *You can't go back*

I can't go on.

> *You must go on. There's no way back.*

But I loved her.

> *I know. I was there.*

Not from the beginning, you weren't.

> *Oh, I know. Just Mom and you.*

Don't sneer. That's just how it was. I want that again.

> *I know you do, we all do—union, nirvana, nothing.*

No. Not nothing. Everything!

> *You wouldn't be you, would you, if you were everything.*
> *You'd be absorbed into somebody else or something*
> *else. Is that what you want? To go back there, to the*
> *womb? If you go forward, you can become yourself,*
> *make yourself.*

I see. So I must go on. To be me.

> *Yes.*

It's scary.

> *Look, I know I was brutal in the beginning, harsh and*
> *cruel. I didn't know how hard it was. I've had to learn,*
> *too. We all want to go back, at times. But we must go*
> *on. And we can. We can do it if we really want to.*

April 14
Sleep

As a child I was often afraid to go to sleep. I felt I was losing control and might even never wake up!

In my addiction, too, I sometimes couldn't sleep—the old fears were still there. I'd lie in bed restlessly, consumed by guilt and shame.

I came to see, as I recovered, that sleep was a time of rest and healing, a deep change from the turbulence of the day.

Now I welcome sleep and I find it a time of integration and gradual change.

> *Yes, I remember how restless we were. And I sneered at you for being a baby—and of course that made things worse. How cruel I was to you, like a sarcastic parent. But that's how I learned to speak to you.*

I know. We both need to change, and then we can be restful together.

April 15
Talking it out

Go on, enjoy yourself. You know I'll love you whatever you do. Just be a child, my child.

You sound like Mother. Always telling me what to do, always knowing more about me than I do myself.

> *You know I'll love you anyway, even if you act out and have fun. Go on, have fun, my love!*

Aren't there any limits, then? Where do I take over?

> *You don't have to, darling. I'm always here.*

Where? Too close. You're stifling me. I want to be free and set my own limits.

> *Why?*

Because I'm not you, I'm me. I want to be myself and set my own boundaries. Listen, I'm getting free of you now.

> *I hate to let you go.*

I know. It's hard. But you've taken over my life. You've set up housekeeping inside me. I need to find my own voice and be my own person.

> *I understand. We both have to learn to be free.*

After making love with my wife, I used to feel a rush of ill will that made a barrier between us.

I tried to give her all my love, but there was always a feeling of distance, unspoken, but present, like a veil between us.

A guy in group said: "Are you there for her, really there?"

Another guy said: "I'm never there when I'm in my addiction. I'm never there for her or for me. I'm only there for it. There's this void, and the addiction. And that's it."

It? The sex addiction.

I checked it out. It was true for me, too. My addiction had taken me away from myself and from my wife. On one side the void, on the other the addiction.

I was absent in my own marriage.

———————

That was it—the moment when you realized you needed help to be in the present of your love and not the absence of your addiction. It was a hard fact to face, but we started working together and we made it. Thank God, we made it!

April 17
Morning

Sleep well?

I sure did. Thanks for asking.

> *Dreams?*

Yes. But good ones. No more nightmares about bodies in bits and pieces.

> *Your porno dreams, you mean?*

Yes. The ones where I was making up bodies from photos and drawings. Building my kit, my kitten, my perfect fantasy woman.

> *That was scary, I remember. She always disintegrated just as you were about to hug her.*

Last night I dreamed I was on my way home and not scared anymore. My wife came out to greet me, and she was real, herself.

> *And then what happened?*

I gave her a hug, and she stayed in my arms. I was home.

> *This sounds real and healthy to me. When we don't squabble and shout, the world doesn't fall apart, even in our dreams.*

When I found out that the basis of my recovery program was spiritual growth, I thought I'd come to the wrong place.

Spirituality was God and God was Church, and Church was what really scared me as a kid, so I thought I'd had enough of that.

Since I liked the people in the group, though, I stayed. They didn't preach at me, and they didn't talk about Church; each of us was free to travel his or her own path.

My sex addiction made me seek only to grab and possess. What I wanted was what I got.

But gradually I began to develop a healthy sexuality that went beyond mere physical coupling. The union that I found went far outside myself and embraced another person and the world.

The path I chose to travel turned out to be the most exciting adventure of them all, an adventure of the spirit.

Yes, you did have a hard time of it at first. Sex was only for you, for your sake. Now we both feel the difference, and what a difference it makes!

April 19
Strife

I'm sick and tired of being a sex addict.

> *Well, that's just exactly what you are and all you are.*

You're one of the causes of my disease, always criticizing and keeping me off balance. I'm sick of you, too.

> *That's because you never listened to me in the first place.*

There, that's typical. Whatever I do or say, I'm in the wrong, according to you. You remind me of my parents, always finding fault and sneering.

> *What are you going to do about it? What can you do?*

I'll tell you. I'm going to join a group and listen to some kinder, more tolerant, and forgiving voices.

> *We'll see.*

Yes, we'll see. You don't have the power over me you used to have. I'm stronger now and can talk in my own voice.

> *I'll be waiting.*

You don't believe in me, do you?

> *Do you?*

Yes. Yes, I do. And I don't have to wait for your approval, either, do I?

> *We'll see. . . .*

I've always loved stories of cheats and crooks who wear disguises and get away with murder.

When Dad left home, I took his place. I had to. Mom clung to me and I tried to be everything for her.

I wanted to grow and grow, all of me, especially my sexual parts, for her.

I'd put on Dad's clothes and look at myself in the mirror. Then I'd undress slowly and wait for the Big Moment.

Rage. Turmoil. Impotence.

She'll never love me. Nobody will.

Mistaken identity.

Is it my fault?

———————

No. You were asked to play a role, but don't forget you've chosen to go on playing it. You've got the insight, now let's work on the recovery. Change the rules and play at being . . . yourself.

April 21
Ripple effect

Last time in group we did "mini-First Steps." We went round the room and each person said why he had come into the program and what it meant to him.

Until then, I'd always talked about my "acting out," but I never said exactly what it was. I was so scared I couldn't name it, because it was hidden under layers of shame.

Then the guy on my left said he was brought up on a farm and he'd had sex with animals. I gasped inside—at his courage.

Then it was my turn. The voices inside me went berserk, and the loudest were those that were the voices of my fear and my shame.

The guy on my left put his hand on my arm.

I said: "My name is Charlie, and I'm a sex addict. I used to have anonymous sex with other men in pornographic bookstores."

> *I feel so proud of that moment and of you. You owned your behavior, you got loving feedback and support, and you're still here, alive and well. Now, our talk is burying that shame!*

Thanks. I need your approval.

I can't stop acting out, I tell you.

> *That's because you're worthless and weak.*

Yes. You're right. I ought to be able to find the power in myself, but I can't.

> *You have no power. You never did have power.*

And I feel so lonely.

> *You'll always be lonely.*

And sad.

> *That's because nobody loves you.*

And evil.

> *Beyond redemption.*

You know, you're just a kind of satanic echo; it's so easy to pull your leg. And I used to believe in your power! I'm going to join a group for sex addicts and find my way to a new source of power. Then I'll take care of you, my friend.

> *You may think you'll find some support in this group of yours. But they'll just laugh at you. And in any case, I certainly won't cooperate. It'll be just one more failure. You'll see.*

April 23
Sin

I feel my sex addiction has made me a sinner beyond any kind of redemption.

> *What about forgiveness?*

The problem is I can't forgive myself.

> *Why not?*

It's the way I've been brought up, I suppose. Guilt and sin and hell fire.

> *Sounds kind of final! Does your group judge and condemn you like that?*

No. And I guess that helps. I feel affection and compassion there. What I need is to learn how to forgive myself.

> *For being human?*

Yes, I know I have to learn to accept that I'm not perfect, and then I can really begin to forgive myself.

> *That sounds healthy to me. Why do we all punish ourselves so much instead of learning to ask for forgiveness and move on? I know we can do better—both of us.*

Most of us need a place we can call our own—a house by the sea, a room with a view, a favorite chair.

We think that when we are there, back home, we will be happy and fulfilled. And often it is so.

But when I am ill at ease, full of contradictory urges, and preparing to act out, I never feel at home wherever I may be.

To be really at home, I need to fill the space that is me with thoughts and feelings that are tranquil and safe.

It takes time to be really at home. But when I am there, I feel in touch with myself and the world around me.

> *Yes, and for a long time you lived only in the wilderness of your sex addiction with its strange, unsettling rituals. And I was always there, another voice keeping you on edge and deep in shame. Now I enjoy the quiet times and rest and home.*

You too?

> *Yes. With you.*

April 25
Bully

I feel like being sexual now that I'm a grown woman.

>*Don't be stupid! You're still a girl.*

I've heard that before—from you, in fact. I'm not listening.
I'm going to be a sexual person in command of her body and
her own life.

>*Don't take any risks.*

How do you mean, risks?

>*Remember what happened to Martha.*

Oh, yes, she got herpes, didn't she? Well, I'll take precautions.

>*You can take all the precautions you want and you can
>still get diseased or pregnant. Besides, have you looked
>at your body lately?*

No. Why? Don't tell me . . .

>*No. Don't worry. It's just that you're ugly.*

That's not what Walt says.

>*He's your brother. He's just trying to make you feel
>good.*

Well, I . . .

>*You are just not made to be sexual.*

Well . . .

>*Your body is ugly, and you're frigid. You'd be better off
>not even thinking of sex. There's plenty to be done in
>the world without sex, you know.*

116

I masturbated like crazy when I was a kid . . . and I mean like crazy. I did it because I was afraid I was going mad, and I was afraid I was going mad because I did it.

I'd lock myself away in my room, and lock myself away from myself. I split my sexual self off, and then I punished it. I was always angry when I masturbated, and even now I still want to masturbate when I'm angry.

I want to control my sexuality; I can't, so I get mad and abuse myself. I want to hurt and demean that part of myself that is sexual because of its power over me.

But then, when I masturbate I feel powerless.

Who's in control, me or my sexuality?

———

Isn't that a false question? Sex is part of us—to be enjoyed, not abused. I know I've been partly responsible for keeping us divided, but let's work together to integrate our life, including our sexuality.

April 27
Envy

Envy splits the self, driving a wedge between love and spite. The envious self exaggerates the value or power of someone else and then gnaws away like a rodent, destroying inner harmony.

Envy often goes hand in hand with sex addiction. The addict, fretful and self-absorbed, envies normal, happy sexuality, even as he flees it.

We can easily become paralyzed by envy, especially if we are full of disgust for ourselves.

As we rejoin the world and learn to work and love and reach out to others, we find that envy, like self-hatred, starts to disappear.

Liking ourselves, we can genuinely like and admire others.

How I used to love to see you, hunched up in the dark corner of your envy! Then I could really increase the pain, by telling you that you were worse than everyone out there, a real toad. But now you're in recovery, we don't need that green-eyed monster of envy anymore.

I want to go out this evening, pick up a guy, bring him home, do some dope, and have some deep, searching sex.

> *Sounds like the same old story to me. Lying old story, too. Boring old, same old, lying old story, in fact.*

Well, that's what you think. But that's what I want.

> *Who wants it?*

I do. I just told you.

> *But which part of you?*

Me, myself, and I.

> *Are you sure it's not just your addicted part?*

Well, what if it is. That's **me,** isn't it?

> *Is that the **you** you want to be?*

Well, if I'm going to be absolutely honest ...

> *Yes?*

No.

> *No?*

No.

> *Let's go on being absolutely honest. It's the only way out of this crazy addiction.*

Yes.

> *Sure?*

Yes.

April 29
Pleasure

I used to think that pleasure was having my own way and going it alone. You know, having fun all the time.

Yes, and to hell with everyone else!

I had this craving in the mouth—for food, for cigarettes, for love.

Love in the mouth?

Yes. A kind of thirst to be kissed and loved to extinction.

Sounds a bit crazy to me.

It was crazy. And I thought I was going crazy, too.

Well, one thing's for sure. You're not crazy now. You're learning.

Yes. I'm learning that pleasure and happiness are two very different things. Happiness involves the mind and the spirit as well as the senses. It's like coming back to sanity, coming home.

Right. And you deserve to feel good about yourself. You were out there in the wilderness far too long. Good to have you back.

And you, Big Daddy?

Oh, sorry, I almost forgot. I'm glad to be back, too!

When my folks raged at each other and even got physical, I ran up to my room and hid.

> *Yes, I remember. You put your hands over your ears and cowered under the bedclothes where it was warm and safe.*

It was like giants hurling rocks, their anger. I couldn't deal with it.

> *Yes, it was foul and wretched. It poisoned life at the source.*

There was nothing for me.

> *Until we found these. Here.*

Yes. I love the smell of the paper. And the gloss, the smoothness.

> *The rustle of the pages.*

Look at that one, the curve and the outline.

> *The seduction and the promise. Go on.*

Yes.

> *Horrors! How could you? You promised. You're sick. You'll never grow up, never make it. You blame everyone except yourself. Little monster. Pervert!*

May 1
Program

Go easy, Dad, you're always on my back.

> *Listen, man, I'm not your dad. That's your problem, your projection.*

Well, you sure talk like him, like God almighty.

> *Aren't you making this up?*

There you go. Next you'll be saying "stupid liar," "warped," "crazy," "pervert."

> *Okay. I know that's what you used to hear when you were a kid. But you're a man now.*

A man. Some hope!

> *So that's it.*

You knew that all the time. You helped keep me scared and weak.

> *Yes, I know I did. But I was programmed, too.*

Programmed? What? Oh, I get it.

> *Our voices come from all kinds of places, some good, some bad. But we can learn to create our own ways of speaking.*

Yes. I'm sorry. I know we can change and I want to.

> *If one voice changes, that makes a whole new dialogue.*

I like that idea. Let's keep talking.

I always seemed to have a rival—in grade school, high school, college, business.

The funny thing was we were always alike in many ways. I mean, why don't I compete with someone different from me?

We were almost the same, my rivals and I, but they always beat me—at schoolwork, sports, business deals, women.

I hated that, yet I loved them, too, in a strange kind of way.

Bob, Jeff, Adam, I can see them now. I wanted to hug them, be them, and yet I detested them for their power.

They were me and not me. Idols.

They were always there in my sexual scenarios. Icons.

And now they're gone, for good.

---

*Bravo! They were your ideal ego, weren't they? Hypnotic, terrifying in their perfection, worshiped yet hated. I'm glad you're back to being **you** again.*

May 3
Manipulation

I nearly always got my way when it came to sex.

> *Yes, you really were the Great Lover.*

All right, don't sneer, you were in it, too.

> *I know. And I was always encouraging you in your exploits so I could sneer and snipe at you later. And anyway it was fun, wasn't it?*

Let's face it, we both went through hell—all that acting out and shouting and screaming. Sometimes I thought my head was going to blow apart.

> *Yes, but all that sex!*

You know it wasn't great. We were lonely and scared.

> *And now?*

I'm not scared now.

> *What's happened? Why are things so different now?*

New power. Higher Power. The group. Community. Love.

> *Yes, that's it. This kind of talk affects me as well as you and helps to keep us changing. That's what it's all about—change and renewal.*

I always wanted to integrate sex into the whole of my life, but I couldn't. It was split off from love and affection and operated as a drug.

Sex for excitement, sex for risk, sex for danger, sex for power, sex for humiliation, sex for debasement—never sex for intimacy or love. I was adrift in loveless sex. I was never **there** for myself or for other people.

Now, in my Twelve Step Program, I am coming in from my heartless and lonely addiction to sex. I talk about it and laugh and grieve, and I strive to surround my sex life with affection and trust.

Sex is becoming integrated into the pattern of my life.

Well done! I must say I never thought you were going to make it and I told you so, just like your dad. But now you're changing, I know it, and I'm changing, too, in my attitude toward you. I feel a new integrity growing between us.

May 5
Out of it

I'm not going to do anything about my addiction.

> *You want to go on as you are now, forever?*

What's wrong with the way I am now?

> *You know very well that you don't act freely in your sexual life. You live in fantasies and act in rituals. You're out of it. Look, I know we can do something about this if we work on it together.*

It's no good talking to me in that reasonable way when my addict is in charge.

> *I suppose you'd prefer the old bullying voice?*

Well, at least I'm used to that.

> *True. What you don't like so much is the voice of reason, isn't that right?*

Why don't you just shut up.

> *You get the point. We need to change voices and roles, you know, and learn from each other. Shouting gets us nowhere. And that's where addiction thrives.*

You know, I'm so lucky to have Sherri for a daughter. I don't even think of her as a daughter, in fact. She's more like a sister. Certainly she's my best friend.

She's going to graduate next June, but she's big for her age. Advanced, really, you know. I tell her everything. I've been lonely since Joe left, but I'm still young, and I'm not a prig. Know what I mean?

Sherri doesn't mind. They're usually gone in the morning. She stays up, often, and we make a threesome. She loves older men.

Once or twice she joined us. Oh, these girls nowadays, they're not shocked by anything. Then next day we sit around and kind of compare notes and have a laugh. Just the two of us.

It brings her real close to me. I need that.

You never had a mother to care for you. It was awful,
stuck out there in Montana with grandma. Sherri's
lucky she's got you. And you're lucky, too. Just the two
of you. It must be so cozy.

May 7
Talk

For as long as I can remember, I've always talked to myself. Sometimes I feel sure that other people can hear what I'm saying to myself—it's so vivid and real!

There are all these voices going around inside my head. Sometimes they all seem to get on well together, like a bunch of friends just chatting around the fire.

But sometimes there's discord and shouting and anger. That's when I want to act out. I can't stand the confusion—one voice is egging me on, another is threatening me, and another keeping me down in my shame.

Since I've been in a Twelve Step group, my voices are kinder and more reasonable. Sometimes they even make me laugh out loud.

I'm learning to like myself, and my voices are responding in kind.

———————————

I'm glad to hear that. And I'm glad to be one of those voices that is becoming kinder and more rational.

When I was a kid at home and asked about sex—silence.

I mean, there were things I really wanted to know, things other kids told me that I didn't understand. Like losing your hair, and Tampax, and getting disease, and girls, and condoms, and on and on.

Silence.

I soon found out for myself I was scared all the time, scared of dirt, sickness, punishment, herpes, God, crabs, Dad, the lot.

No answer.

Mom gave me a book one day . . . left it on my bed. It was just as the kids had said—disease, filth, insanity, even death.

I asked my parents about it one day, after dinner, just some of the things I wanted to know.

Mom said: "I gave you that book."

Silence.

> *And then I took over, scolding and slandering and threatening. Disease and madness. Punishment and hell.*

I think we're still in it.

> *No, we're talking now, not shouting.*

That's true. And in the quiet we can hear ourselves think.

May 9
Trouble

In my group, I meet people who have been rejected by spouses and friends, arrested, forbidden to see their children, beaten up, ostracized, sent to prison—all because of their sex addiction.

The life of a sex addict is full of pain, fear, danger, perhaps violence. The sick thrill of the risk is part of the attraction—but what a price to pay!

I won't pay that price anymore. The risks I want to take are the risks of happiness, of intimacy, of commitment.

That's where I am and that's going to be my life.

I'm glad you have the courage to say that. When you were acting out, the risks you took weren't courageous, just dangerous and self-destructive.

I know. I just said that!

Sorry. I'm being smug again.

Thanks for seeing that.

Thanks for saying that.

I see all these images and articles about Modern Woman and I freak out.

> *How come?*

Because she's such a fantastic creature, like three myths in one—Athena the Wise One, Artemis the daring one, and Venus the sexy one. She's running the office, taking risks in her personal life, and having utterly delirious orgasms.

> *Not all at once, surely?*

Almost. Or at least on the same day. Sometimes even three times a day. And look at me!

> *Well, what about you?*

A nobody in the office, always playing it safe, and two orgasms a month if I'm lucky.

> *Yes. I know it's hard. But do you really think we all have to be like people in magazines or on that trivial little screen? Most of it's hype, you know that?*

I suppose so. But it does put women down, in a subtle way. Just like the old days—whatever you were, whatever you did, it was never enough. I just want to be content to be myself.

> *And you're not?*

No. I'm not.

> *I know it's hard. And often I'm carping and complaining about you, too. I do see your point. Let's stop being goddesses and start being human.*

May 11
Other people

As an addict I saw other people as objects of desire and lust. How could we get together, quickly, and get it on?

No time for friendship, tenderness, affection, curiosity, intimacy, warmth. Just the swift search for **my** pleasure, **my** gratification.

The morning after always brought loneliness and shame. Where was the pleasure I had so desperately been seeking? Where, even, was the other person?

My addiction caused me to abuse other people, turning them into empty shadows in a world of fantasy and lust.

Then came the First Step and a new power base. My life filled with projects, real friendships, openness, peace.

I have come to see other people as people, not shadows.

> *Well, it took you a while. No, that's mean. I was to blame, too. I did nothing to help, in the beginning. I needed to change, as well.*

Now we can be in a healthy relationship at last.

There are some words I hate to look at and hate to hear.

Such as?

Homosexual.

Let's talk about it.

When I see that word on a page, it jumps out at me and makes me feel sick.

Why's that?

I used to think "homo" meant "perverted," or "queer."

What does it mean?

It means "like," "similar." It means you want to be sexual with someone like yourself.

Is that so terrible?

Yes. No. I don't know. I mean, I really hate those faggots you see around campus these days.

Why?

They scare me. They make me feel violent. I hate them.

Because you're afraid you might be "like" them, and even, deep down, want to love someone "like" yourself?

Yes. I've never even dared think that thought. But that's it. Yes.

I know all your life you've been taught to fear and hate those "faggots." But now that you see all sexuality as human, maybe you can come to terms with your own feelings about homosexuality. You'll like yourself better when you do so.

May 13
Hard core

I know some feminists are against it, but I want to see sexual violence between women on the screen. I'm fed up with all that fuzzy romance and pastel flesh. I like strong women and I crave force.

What do you crave about it?

I even love the word. And I like to see the anger and the fear and feel the lash of brutality. I'm there, on the receiving end.

Do you deserve it?

Sure. And I like it, too.

Seems to me you're a bit too sure, a bit strident. What are you hiding?

Nothing.

Are you sure? Trust me.

I'm scared, scared at being laughed at, demeaned.

By whom?

You. All those voices. Everyone.

Can't we start to change all that? I know you've been lonely—me too. Now we've admitted it, let's do something about it.

Like what?

Like working together and rewriting our life.

Sex was a way of not being myself—a sort of reprieve from the job of living.

When things got rough, I took time out for myself, and ran off to the porno videos.

The thing is, the more I went, the less I enjoyed it. It wasn't a reprieve, just an escape. Escape from misery into misery.

And then one day, suddenly, I said to myself, "You know, you don't need this. It's wrecking your work, yourself, your family."

I was creating a new voice, one that was positive and supportive. A new voice that was clear and calm and determined.

And that's the voice I'm going to listen to when the going gets rough.

Yes. It sure is a new voice and it's coming through loud and clear. Now we can really talk like grown-up people.

I feel the change in both of us.

*That's because we **are** changing, both of us.*

May 15
Rigid

I feel great after that meeting. I learned so much about myself just listening to the others and then joining in, for me.

> *I felt left out.*

How come?

> *Nobody talked about plans or schemes. It seemed so loose and formless.*

And you love things fixed and rigid.

> *Am I rigid, hidebound?*

Sometimes you're as uptight as a constipated Victorian magistrate. Is it so hard to relax a bit and let things happen?

> *Let it all hang out, you mean? Do your own thing. Get mellow, man. Go with the flow. I hate all that hippie-yuppie stuff!*

No. I didn't say that. I mean tolerant, flexible, open. That doesn't deny values, does it?

> *No, I guess not. But isn't it scary not to go by the book?*

Yes. A bit. But there are books and there's life. They aren't the same, are they?

> *I suppose not.*

Let's see what we can do about living . . . together.

From obsession to compulsion is only a short step. First the fantasies and then the acting out.

In fantasy I'd create the magic scenario and then, of course, I'd have to go and test it out. It was never what I really wanted and I'd fall back again into disgust and despair.

And then the fantasies again—to escape the pain. And on and on.

Break free! That's what I wanted, but I couldn't do it alone. I needed new power and support.

That's where the Program came in. I began to take steps away from compulsion and toward a free and honest life.

It took a while, didn't it? And I was always there to make it hard for you—the old, harsh voice from the past. Now I can't beat you up anymore, you're too strong. And that makes life easier for all of us!

May 17
Commitment

Gays are supposed to do it all the time, every night a new partner. At least that's what they told me when I came out and admitted my sexual preference.

And, was I miserable! Always cruising, always looking for that ideal adventure on the unreal lovemap of my fantasies.

It took me a while to sober up, and I could never have done it without my Twelve Step group. I had to reach inside myself and seek out the addiction that was driving me crazy. Admit my powerlessness and the depths of my despair.

And then the work of healing. It's been a long time and a hard road, but I've never been alone since the day I joined the group. We're all committed to each other and to the journey of recovery.

That's the map of my life now, complex and exciting and real, and it's exactly where I want to be right now.

> *Good. I'm with you all the way. I'm really committed to our recovery and I like you as you are.*

Just as I am? Are you sure?

> *Sure.*

Off to meet one of our new lover boys, are we?

There you go again, sneering and jeering.

> *Can't you take a joke?*

It's not a joke when you repeat it every other day.

> *Well, you seem to have a new lover every other day. Just kidding.*

Just kidding! Just kidding! Just like Dad, treating me like a little doll! "Only kidding, sweetie!" Look, I'm a grown-up person . . . we both are . . . let's get together instead of always being at odds.

> *Okay. I guess we need each other, all of us. If only our voices could tune in to each another, we'd get somewhere, be someone.*

That's right. And anyway, we **are** getting somewhere, just talking like this. Getting to understand each other. We **are** someone. But it's hard to get all these voices together.

> *Yes, I know. But let's keep on talking. I'm learning that it's no fun being the angry parent all the time. I'd like to be an adult, too, you know.*

Keep trying, Dad.

> *Thanks, kid.*

May 19
Divorce

When my parents were divorced, I felt guilty.

I'd already started acting to escape from all the hurt and fighting. I thought that my father knew about it and couldn't stand to live with his evil little daughter. So he left.

I hardly ever saw him again for years. And then one day I went and stayed with him for a week, and he gave me a book about sex addiction.

I read and I was scared at first. He knew!

But then he told me that he had been a sex addict and had lots of affairs when he was living with us. He asked me how that had affected me.

"I became a sex addict, too."

Finally it was there between us, our lonely secret. We hugged and wept and talked and talked.

That was a great moment. Of course I had to change my attitude toward you, and that was hard. I was so used to being the wounded and reproachful mother. It's great that we all can keep on changing.

I used to fool around with a guy at school who had a whole stack of his dad's pornography in his basement room.

We'd sit there for hours and stare and fantasize. Then he told me about a girl in the neighborhood who always left her window open and undressed, it seemed, for hours.

And then, of course, we watched her for hours, too, outside in the rain, hot and clammy, staring and whispering and giggling. Nothing wrong in that, I suppose, is there?

And then one day I saw her folks leave and I ran to her window and knocked. She turned and stared and I exposed myself to her, in a flash.

And after that, I had to have people look at me, and then came the porno shops and furtive anonymous acts.

It's been like that for years, until finally I just had to find help.

Yes, I know, I was there, and not on your side. We did give each other a hard time, I know. But I'm here for you now, and I can see the changes as we work the Program. That old split between us is slowly healing.

May 21
Flight

Well that was good while it lasted, but it's time to move on.

> *Yes, you've had the best of her.*

You know, she's attractive, but, well, I don't know. . . .

> *Dumb?*

Well, not exactly, but you know, I do have a 3.7 grade average.

> *Exactly. You need someone you can talk to. Someone smart.*

Sure. But, remember that dark one, three or four months back. She was smart and fun.

> *And you left her, too.*

I leave them all. . . .

> *Before they leave you.*

Looks that way, doesn't it?

> *It is that way. Is that what you really want?*

No.

> *Well, that's quite an admission. Let's build on that little word. It came from the heart, and that's the right place to start.*

Yes. I used to be scared of the heart.

> *That's where the answers are.*

And the questions?

> *The questions, too.*

I know that when I was a kid, love was blocked between my parents and me. They demanded my love and left me no choice.

They didn't want love, they wanted admiration and obedience on their terms. I felt like a slave.

And so, I acted out, just to show them. I was saying, "I want to be free, to be me," but I just became enslaved to my addiction. In a twisted way, my parents were still there, in my acting out.

Was I reaching out or running away? I'll probably never know. I used to see my mother's face behind the pornography, and I was glad, and yet I grieved for her. She was still there, another picture.

But now I've been able to make my peace with my parents. I see them as people, not just images and voices.

I had to find my own voice before I could speak to them. Freely.

Well, that's change, if you like. And my voice has changed too, have you noticed? Now I can be an adult, and not just a parent.

May 23
Network

People say the brain is a network of pathways, rather like a map. Nothing ever disappears; all the traces of my life are there.

Some of those traces went off in strange directions in my childhood, and when I reconnected with them, they brought me thrills and pain. I feared to go there, and yet I always went back, addicted to those weird sexual byways.

I wasn't born that way, I know. It just happened. I don't feel responsible, and yet I do have the need to get well. And that's what's happening in my Twelve Step Program.

I'm creating new traces, new pathways. And now when the old urge comes, I have other options, other tracks. And that feels good.

> *I liked it when you were lost, I must admit.*

How come?

> *It was easy for me to sneer at you and feel superior.*

And what's different now?

> *You're different. Me too. And that's quite a difference!*

I used to feel powerless because I had been taught to hate my body and my sexual organs.

I'd look at myself in the mirror and try and imagine someone finding me attractive as a woman. Not a hope!

So I turned to images and videos for sexual release—at least **they** couldn't look back at me and despise me. What a sick feeling of power that gave me!

Now I can laugh at those childish fears. The Program has brought me to see myself in a new light, the light of affection and tolerance. My friends in the group have helped me to see that I wasn't crazy—just blind.

Blind to the value that is in each and every one of us.

> *I was really working against you and laughed at your skinny body and ugly face. Why was that? I took over for other people and brought their imagined scorn inside. Well, that just doesn't work anymore, thank heavens.*

And thanks to us and our Program.

May 25
Victim

You know the story of the sadist and the masochist?

> *Tell me.*

The masochist says "Whip me! Whip me!" And the sadist just sits there and looks and sits there and then says in a slow, harsh, shuddering voice: "No. No. No."

> *So?*

That's how we were, you and I. I felt I deserved to be punished, I don't know why. I hadn't **done** anything, it's just that I enjoyed the humiliation and the pain. And you'd just sit there and let me stew in my own juice.

> *Yes, and I guess I enjoyed that, too. It was a way of keeping you in my power, and power's what I was mad for.*

God. What crazy days those were, crazy and miserable. I'm glad we've come through and can talk now like old friends.

> *Yes. And you know, you're a really neat person now that you've stopped being a victim.*

And you? What about you?

> *I feel better, too. Where's my whip?*

I threw it in the lake.

I used to allow myself to be beaten up by a voice that told me I was worthless and corrupt.

That voice was part of me, and yet it seemed to come from outside and from the past.

As I recovered from my sex addiction I became stronger and more confident. I learned to resist that voice and fight clear of it.

And then I found it had no power over me anymore. Now when it talks to me, it is gentler and encouraging.

I'm finally getting myself together.

> *Yes, you're right. My voice was a harsh and hating voice, but that was partly because you hated yourself. Now you're getting healthy and strong and there's no need for us to live in fear of self-division and strife.*

Yes, that's it. Getting **myself** together is unifying the **two** of us.

May 27
Zipless

I thought it was great in the sixties and seventies when sex was an everyday occurrence and zippers were for old fogies.

I mean, after all those years of repression and anxiety, we were the Free and Easy Women, into our bodies and ourselves.

We read all those famous books and acted them out in our lives.

Or tried to.

Maybe my friends and I went about it the wrong way, or maybe we didn't understand those books. Or maybe the people who wrote the books just had the experience . . . of writing books.

Whatever.

The fact is that I slept around a lot and I still do. I still want to fly and get high.

But it doesn't feel like freedom.

> *It sounds like addiction to me.*

It feels like addiction.

> *Want to do something about it?*

I think so. Yes. Yes.

Sometimes I still feel tempted to go to the places where I used to act out . . . just to see, just to remember, just to check things out. And of course, once I'm there, why not . . . just this once?

Sex addiction is not something to play around with; it's an affliction with a long history and a long memory.

There are other ways of checking things out—making a phone call to a friend, talking to my sponsor, doing a Step, reading a meditation, letting in some fresh ideas.

I'm far better off checking things out in my Program and keeping to the path of sanity.

> *I used to egg you on, of course, and then, if you had a slip, I'd be there to sneer and humiliate you. Well, you set yourself up, didn't you?*

Still blaming and shaming, Mr. Superdad!

> *Sorry. Let's leave the past alone.*

And live in the present.

May 29
Degradation

*C*ome on, let's have a real talk.

What about?

> *You don't have to be so defensive.*

I don't like your tone.

> *Tone, tone, tone! Why don't you listen to what I'm actually saying!*

Your tone gets in the way, that's why. I've listened to that voice all my life. It started when I was a kid and it hasn't changed one bit.

> *That's because you haven't changed yourself. Why don't you try?*

Same old crap! Try, try, try. That means you're saying "Why don't you do what I want!"

> *All right, baby, have it your own way.*

I shall, for once.

> *For once! That's what you always do—have things your own way. That's why you'll always be an addict.*

I used to think I was never really there. I mean, often it was as if I had no center, no reality.

When I acted out, it was as if someone else were in charge.

And so I denied that I was responsible for my acts; I'd say, "It was my addict." I felt like a Jekyll-and-Hyde person, split in half between good and evil.

Now, in recovery, I've developed a new sense of myself. My group has helped me find a way to affirm my identity, and the program makes me feel good to be me.

I don't feel the need for that tired old addict anymore. He's the absent one now.

> *Well, I'm glad to hear that! Whenever you did something you didn't like, you always blamed your addict. And I always jumped on you for that.*

You loved doing that, didn't you?

> *Yes. But we can all change, can't we?*

Even you, Granddad?

> *Even me.*

May 31
Pit stop

You know, sex for me used to be like those racing cars that pull in for a quick fix—a trip to the pit stop.

I'd drop in to the bookstore or to a lover's house, just to top up—and then I'd bottom out. Lonely, down, full of self-contempt and hatred. I knew that what I was doing was destructive and yet I couldn't stop. I needed the gas just to keep in the race.

I really did bottom out. Drugs, a suicide attempt, the whole thing.

And then this guy told me about a Twelve Step group. I laughed, of course, and said I'd rather go it alone. And he said, "well, you're alone all right, and there won't be anyone at your funeral if you go on like this."

That was a brutal picture—the rain, the damp, stark trees, no birds singing, a coffin, and nobody there to remember and mourn.

Well, okay, I'd drop in, just to see. And I found, here in my group, what I'd always been looking for—warmth, openness, caring, and love in abundance.

Yes, you were in a really bad way. And we were at war, you and I, and that sure didn't help. Things are different now. It seems like a miracle, and it works every day. Let's keep going back!

I don't just live, do I?

> *How do you mean?*

I mean, I'm really an operator, working on a high-powered, self-centered seduction system.

> *Wow. That's quite a mouthful. But I have to admit, it's true.*

Every time I want sex I can always justify it by appealing to my system. I just plug in to all those clichés.

> *True.*

Like, "I need sex." "I feel powerful when I get someone to go to bed." "I deserve some fun." "She was asking for it," and on and on.

> *Yes. I recognize all those tired old voices. And I'm tired of them too. What's your plan?*

Change voices, change systems, change behaviors.

> *That's a lot of changing all at once.*

Are you doubting me?

> *No. But we can take it a day at a time.*

153

June 2
Interdependence

I used to hate relying on people—they always asked too much or let me down.

Anyway, I felt proud to be a loner. I loved the idea that nobody knew about my secret fantasies and acting out with prostitutes. It gave me a sense of power.

Some power! In reality, I was only covering up for my loneliness and self-hatred and lack of trust.

When trust came back, in my Twelve Step Program, I felt ready to reach out and connect with others in the group.

I learned to count on them and trust them, and they returned my trust in full measure.

We need one another, and we can say that proudly, out loud.

> *And what about me?*

Poor little Supervoice, how sad you sound!

> *I have needs, too, you know.*

We both do. Let's help each other and not be afraid anymore.

As a child I felt I could never do anything right. Dad would say: "Why can't you grow up and be more like your mother?"

I was clumsy, and it got worse. Mom would say, "Why don't you watch what you're doing?" "What's wrong with you? You're never really here."

A girl I knew was into sex games with some kids on the block. I joined their secret society. We'd have "orghies," as we called them, in her dad's barn.

I couldn't keep away from them. There were boys as well as us girls. Then one day one of the girls taught me how to give myself an orgasm.

It was incredible. Another world. I did it all the time—I called it "going to the barn."

It was wild and scary, but it was mine.

When things get tough, I always "go to the barn."

Yes, you still do, all the time. Does it really help, especially when the going gets rough? Sometimes I wonder if we'll ever take the risk of a real sexual relationship . . . with someone else. Can we talk about that, quietly?

June 4
Ritual

After a while my acting out became as predictable as any formal ceremony.

I would start by looking at pornographic pictures. Then I would gaze at my body in the mirror. Then the careful dressing-up, cloaking my male body in female garments. Then out into the dark streets to look for furtive, anonymous sex.

It's hard, even now, to say these things and to own them. And yet each time I speak to a friend or in my group, the pain and the shame diminish.

Now when I feel the ritual beginning, I can break the spell by reaching for the phone or talking kindly to myself.

Words help, words heal—and that's good to know.

> *That's right. Before, we were always "having words," because we were at war with each other. Now we can talk things over together.*

Yes. And I'm even beginning to respect you, old man.

> *Well, don't I deserve it, dear boy?*

June 5
Making an end

You know this business of making amends to people is confusing me. I went to see a guy I had harmed through my sex addiction, and I asked him what I could do to make things up to him, and he said, "Come to bed with me." So I did.

> *You don't have to be quite so literal about it, you know. And the Ninth Step does say. . . .*

I know what the Ninth Step says.

> *Well, do you know what the Ninth Step means?*

I guess not.

> *Well it doesn't mean you have to go around and sleep with people you've harmed by going around sleeping with them. Otherwise. . . .*

There'd be no end to it, would there?

> *Right. Making amends implies making an end . . . to destructive behavior.*

And being sorry.

> *Yes.*

I really am sorry.

> *Yes, I know you are. Me too.*

June 6
Fusion

I hate you. You've always kept me away.

> *From what?*

From wanting to be myself, the child I never was.

> *But isn't that a fiction, a make-believe?*

Who? What?

> *That lovely child, gorgeous image, ideal ego.*

You see. Always putting me down, keeping me apart. The same as when I was a child. All I wanted was to be what I most admired. And I still want that. What's wrong with that?

> *What about yourself, you as you really are? Isn't that enough?*

I'm too different. Odd.

> *That's what makes you **you**.*

What?

> *Difference.*

I don't know. I'll see. Perhaps we can work on it together.

> *Yes. If we can join forces in the real world, we can break the magic spell and smash that gorgeous childish mirror. Look, you're here, alive, human.*

Acting out is not a positive act but a reaction: addiction is a response to the desert of loneliness and pain.

I get angry or afraid or depressed or sad, and instead of coping with the feelings, I act out. When I do that, sex is a reflex, not a true act of love.

I need to be attentive to this trigger mechanism and learn to act in a positive way at the critical moment. I can call a friend or read a passage from my meditations, or talk to myself kindly, or simply feed the cat.

Then I will find myself acting, instead of acting out.

> *I'll help too by giving you positive messages instead of the old criticism and scorn.*

That would be a welcome change.

> *I know. But don't forget we're both changing now.*

You too?

> *Can you believe it?*

Yes.

June 8
Underground

Feelings, feelings, feelings . . . I'm sick and tired of feelings.
Today in the group that's all we talked about.

> *And you didn't say a word.*

I just told you. I'm sick of feelings.

> *But you never talk about **your** feelings.*

I don't know how, that's why. You can't **just suddenly** talk
about your feelings.

> *I didn't say "just suddenly." I know it takes time, and
> practice.*

Practice? It's not a game of golf!

> *Yes. Practice. At home we never learned. Everything
> was underground, hidden, dark, secret.*

Shut up.

> *Everything was as secret as sex. As tangled as sex. As
> dark as sex.*

I can't stand this. I can't! I can't! I can't!

> *I'm here. Hold on. I want to be helpful. We have to
> trust each other and learn to talk our way through to
> feelings, yes, and even secrets. Even sex!*

I thought I could manage sex, but it managed me. It came at all times of the day and night, unbidden and unannounced, and threatened to take over my life.

How did this distortion happen, when did it start? I don't know—and maybe I'll never know.

The main thing is to realize that, when sex manages me, I'm an addict and powerless to control my life.

I have to feel powerless because as an addict **I am powerless to go it alone.** I need a different energy, new relationships, another source of power than my puny ego.

It's there for me when I need it. It's there in my group and the Twelve Step Program. And it's there for everyone who wants to find it.

Now you're talking! I can hear the strength in your voice. The strength of the group and not just the ego.

161

Messages

Sex is impersonal. Sex is exploitation. Sex is power.

> *Sex is intimate, trusting, open-minded.*

Sex is secretive, dirty, shameful.

> *Sex is the blaze of life.*

Sex is pictures, not life, bodies, not people. Sex is a prowling, prying, peeping, raping camera.

> *Sex is a world of knowledge and pleasure shared in intimacy.*

Sex is denial and refusal.

> *Sex opens out to the world in affirmation.*

I want to believe that, but I can't.

> *Talk about it.*

I can't.

> *Gently does it. Each time we go to the group, I feel you are closer to your feelings and closer to new words of healing. Have faith in your Higher Power; the words do come when you are ready.*

In my addiction I used to spend all my energy fantasizing and acting out. At the end of the day I was exhausted, even though I'd accomplished very little.

Thinking of sex, creating images, pursuing phantoms—all that takes time and energy and leaves me nothing left for work or friends.

When I began my Program and stopped acting out, I gradually found new sources of energy and a new love of life.

It was hard at first; but, like anything else, if I take it one day at a time, I find I can keep going.

Practice doesn't make perfect; we will never be perfect, but as we strive to recover, our energy and zest for life expand. Now we have time and power to live and love.

Yes, that's it. And I have to spend less energy beating you up. The tension between us, inside of us, kept us agitated and isolated. Now we can move on, out into the world.

June 12
Buried alive

It's funny, I can read a page of my medical textbook and remember nearly all of it. They say I have a photographic memory. But my childhood . . . nothing.

> *I know. Sometimes it's as if we never had a childhood. Maybe we were born at five.*

Yes! That was it. No. Not born. Found!

> *Like Moses, yes! Down by the pond.*

Yes. Not born. Found! Found by the water. Born from the water, perhaps—yes, born from the foam of the water, born from the clear beauty of the water, like Venus!

> *Yes. Like Venus! Not born from parents or people.*

Not born from sex.

> *Horrible, violent, mutilating sex.*

Dirty sex, stinky sex, filthy sex—down **there.**

> *Vile and violent. Ugh! How can you even think of it?*

I can't. Forget it.

> *I can't forget it. Heaven and earth, must I remember! That noise, that screaming, that filth, that violence. No. No. No. No sex. No childhood. Nothing.*

"Just love me a little while longer and help me with my life.
I can't do it alone, you have to be there for me, to cure me, to
make me whole."

That's how I used to speak and write to my beloved, my muse,
my nurse, my mother! I wanted someone else to heal the
wound, to close the gap that separated me from a feeling of
primal Oneness.

Maybe we can never be whole, complete, totally unified and
fulfilled. Perhaps it's part of our sorrow and our strength to
realize that we are imperfect, flawed, always striving to live
as best we can.

Yes, that's it. And now I can stop looking for that missing part
inside or outside myself, stop longing for a perfect unity that
exists only in my fantasy.

To be a part doesn't mean living apart. If I recognize my own
incompleteness and imperfections, then I can be proud to be
part of a truly human community.

> *You and your perfectionism! How hard it was to just be,
> with all that nonsense running through your head. All
> that made it difficult for anyone else to love you. I'm
> glad you're finally content to be just you.*

You sound a bit distant, like a wise old man.

> *Sorry. I want to love you, as a friend.*

Thanks, friend.

June 14
Coming out

*T*hat was a good talk in the group today, wasn't it?

Yes. I was amazed.

>   *About what, especially?*

The way Sharon talked about sex. So open and frank.

>   *I agree. Why can't we do that?*

Because we never learned. In the family it was always taboo.
And at school everyone blushed and giggled about it. And
then Mom always worried about me and sex and disease.

>   *Yes. And I took over Mom's voice when she died. Poor
>   old Mom, scared and rigid. And you were the fragile
>   little girl.*

Well, it doesn't always have to be like that, does it? I mean we
can learn from Sharon and the others.

>   *Learn? Change? Sounds scary.*

Yes. But we can do it.

>   *I suppose we can. But you'll have to be patient with me,
>   you know. I've been programmed to be the inflexible
>   parent, always on guard like a sentry. But I can change
>   if we work together on it. And I want to. Wouldn't it be
>   great to be out in the open, like Sharon?*

I was doing so well, really working my program, feeling in touch with myself and the guys in the group, enjoying my work, getting along well with my wife . . . and then wham! A slip.

Not just a little slip. A full-blown affair when I was off at a convention in Atlanta.

I came home mortified. I couldn't look Shelly, my wife, in the eye. I think she knew, somehow, but didn't want to hear. She said, "Well, it's good you're back. You probably missed your group."

Did I ever! And when I owned my slip, the guys were really supportive and understanding. They helped me not to beat myself up. "Move forward; don't look back," they said.

And now I'm back on track again.

It's going to work. It's working!

> *Yes. It's fine. And it's good to hear you being so affirmative about yourself and the Program. And, by the way, don't forget you're human!*

You, too, my dear old Supervoice!

June 16
The long run

*W*hy *do you have to keep on acting out?*
I like the thrill of it.

    Getting out of yourself?
Yes. Going beyond. Getting high.

    How long does it last?
Well, that's the trouble.

    Trouble?
It doesn't last. Not long, anyway.

    And is it worth it?
Worth it?

    In the long run.
The long run? Well, when I'm really being honest with
myself, I guess I don't think it's worth it. In the long run. But
there's something there, something in the moment that I want,
that I crave. It's the edge.

    Razor's edge?
Ouch! Yes, I know it's dangerous. But what can I do?

    *What can we do? Talk. Keep going to our group. Work
    the Program. I need it, too, you know. We both do.*

Whenever I wanted sex I convinced myself that the other person was available and willing—open for business, day or night.

For me the fantasy was the act, and the image, the person. I never stopped to wonder about freedom or responsibility.

I treated people like porno magazines, and then I discarded them.

Working in my group has shown me that we all need to own our desires and choices. Women, especially, have claimed their rights to be treated as people, not objects.

Sex is a gift, not a demand or a threat.

> *That's news to me!*

Well, you can learn too, you know.

> *From you?*

From me.

June 18
Small talk

I want to go off and get high on sex again.

> *Of course you do, but you can't.*

Why not? You're not my boss.

> *Oh yes I am. You gave me that power.*

No! You took it.

> *See, you admit it. I've got the power. You're just a
> feeble slob.*

Wait, don't think this voice of yours is here forever. I have
other resources now, and other choices. I don't even want to
go leering at women and showing off. I'm beginning to be
content to be me.

> *Sounds phony to me.*

No, it's real, and I'm putting an end to this childish small talk
of ours. From now on let's have an adult conversation, shall
we?

> *Yes. I'm tired of the hassle, too. I'm just repeating the
> old stuff to see if it works. And I can see we're in a new
> relationship now. If we stick together, we can keep on
> talking sense.*

I used to think that seduction was just connected with getting someone to go to bed with you. But now I know better.

In my alcoholism recovery group there are a couple of men who have just joined the Program. They met each other in another group about six months ago.

They come on very strong. When one of us is struggling with boundaries, they laugh and say that there's nothing wrong with masturbation . . . "in fact it prevents your drying up and withering away."

Last week they were both in my small group. I needed to talk about my acting out with older men, and one of them joked about it in an inappropriate way and the other one nodded and winked at me.

They've never made a pass at me, but they take pleasure in undermining the way I feel about myself.

They want to bring me down to their level in a degrading kind of way.

I don't need this right now.

Good for you! I used to do that kind of thing to you myself in the bad old days. I'm glad you're speaking up about this. I think we should change groups and find one just for women, for a while. At this point, we need all the strength and support we can get.

June 20
Impasse

I want to live . . . to live in the moment.

> *Even if it means acting on impulse?*

Yes. Why not? We only live once!

> *Do you call sex addiction living?*

I'm talking about sex, not addiction. What's wrong with sex?

> *But it's not just sex. You know that. In your case, it's addiction.*

You keep telling me that. I'd never even heard of the word "addiction" until you started bugging me with it.

> *It's for your own good.*

I know what's good for me, Big Daddy. The present is where I'm at, where I want to be. We're all going to die, you know.

> *Do you want to die an addict?*

Addict! Addict! Addict! Is that all you can think about?

> *You're really on the defensive. We'll never get anywhere if we go on like this.*

172

I used to have my favorite sexual scenarios and I'd act them out again and again, like a ritual.

I thought I was free to choose the actors and the setting; but now I realize that I was stuck there like a sleepwalker.

I was in a trance each time I acted out, and I couldn't get on with my life and relate to other people.

A therapist told me that a fixation is a failure to translate something from the unconscious—a kind of verbal breakdown. Then the unconscious takes over and causes me to spin my wheels.

I think I'm going somewhere, but I always stay in the same place. Not acting; just acting out.

I had to learn to talk my way out of the past and into the present. Only then could I really get on with my life.

> *Yes, you didn't talk much in the old days—you were too busy locked in your own thoughts. It was I who did all the talking, blaming and shaming you. Now you really are talking, and what you say makes sense to both of us.*

We're both changing, and what a joy that is!

June 22
Out in the open

I want to lie down, let go, and make love to myself.
>*Why not, then?*

Because I don't even like myself.
>*So?*

So I get mad and want to demean myself, even hurt myself.
>*Do you feel ashamed of wanting to masturbate?*

Yes, all the time.
>*Well, how about a bit of abstinence until you feel better
>about yourself?*

And then what?
>*And then you can choose for yourself. Out in the open.*

But I thought you were always telling me it's wrong, wrong,
wrong.
>*That was Mom's voice. I'm changing, haven't you
>noticed?*

Well. . . .
>*Really, haven't you noticed?*

Yes. And I'm glad.
>*Me too. Maybe I shouldn't always have the last word.
>I'm sure I don't really, anyway, do I? Let's keep on
>talking. It's so good to know we're both on the move,
>changing.*

Yes. On the move, together.

I remember the dark and then the body sliding into bed with me when I was a kid.

The whispers and the groping. My brother's pleading and triumph.

The pain and the release. The fear and the thrill. I can't forget the thrill.

It was a sick thrill, the same kind I get now when I act out.

But it is a thrill—the unknown, the risk, the danger.

And the disease, I can't forget that. And the shame and disgust. And the anonymity, the lack of real human touch.

And the pain.

It's crazy, I know. If only I could stop. But do I really want to?

No. And anyway, I can't.

> *Hey! I'm here. All that stuff sounds kind of final, and not very sensible, come to think of it. Those crazy voices, that endless hubbub, that torment!*

I know. It's hurtful, deadly.

> *For both of us. But if we pick out the sane moments and the healthy voices, we can start building a new place to be.*

June 24
Separation

You know what I feel like when I see monkeys picking at their fleas?

No. Tell me.

I feel anxious.

Because you might get fleas?

No. Because I think it's a sign of separation anxiety.

Separation from whom?

From their mother. The monkeys' mother I mean.

And why do you feel anxious when you see the monkeys picking at their fleas?

Because I want my mother. I know it's ridiculous . . . here I am, a forty-five-year-old doctor, and when I see monkeys picking at their fleas, I feel homesick . . . for my mother.

Well, I'm glad we can talk about it.

Yes, I'm really glad we can talk about it now. In the old days . . .

Yes.

I'd have acted out.

I know. And that's the great step forward . . . to be able to talk about anxiety instead of letting it drive you to those dreary old porno bookstores.

I was brought up to think that doing is more important than being. At home, at school, in business, what counted was success and getting ahead.

I was supposed to be a success story, not a person. And everything I did contributed to that fiction—the fiction of the "self-made man."

But we're not "self-made"; we are shaped and moved by all of our interactions with all kinds of people in all kinds of settings.

When we change systems, from a system of addiction to a program of recovery, we find we are in a place where what matters is who we are.

Who we are, not what we've done. And that helps us live a full life as a human being.

> *That sounds so beautiful. But isn't who we are connected to what we've done?*

Yes, of course, the two are connected. But we are more than the sum of our acts, don't you think? We must be, surely. Otherwise . . .

> *You sound anxious. We need to talk more about this.*

June 26
Tomorrow

I can quit, I know I can.
>*When?*

Tomorrow.
>*Sure?*

You'll know tomorrow.
>*That's what you said yesterday, you know.*

Did I? Well, I meant it.
>*But today's tomorrow, from the point of view of yesterday.*

I see what you mean. Okay, today. Let's go to that group we were talking about.
>*Which group?*

Okay. I deserved that. You remember, the one we talked about yesterday!
>*Great! If we keep talking this thing over in a friendly way, we'll start getting somewhere.*

When?
>*Now.*

I used to think women belonged to me—at least those women I stayed with for more than a couple of months.

I was the piper and they had to dance to my tune. Otherwise I just dumped them.

I told them I wasn't ready for commitment, but I wasn't ready for equality, either, or affection, or love.

The fact is that I was frightened—frightened of women, frightened of their bodies, frightened of sex.

I had to find a way of talking about this, and it had to be a safe place where my fears would be listened to and understood. That's why I joined a Twelve Step group where people have been through the same kinds of fears and feelings of inadequacy.

I'm in a safe place now, at home with myself. The old fears have gone.

Finally I feel self-possessed and ready for a real adult relationship.

Good. I was scared too, and that's why I spent my time being angry at you and keeping you on edge. Fear breeds anger and then more fear. I'm glad we've come through to a quieter, safer place.

June 28
The big question

In the sad loneliness of my addiction I spent hours and hours out in the cold, on tiptoe, peeping.

I know. What did you want to see?

Everything. Women. Life. The Truth.

Oh, the Big Things, eh? And I thought it was just sex.

It's never "just sex." There's always something more. Sex is the beginning, the arc, the portal, the gateway.

How come?

Because sex takes you beyond into the Beyond. Sex is the Mystery, the Breakthrough, the Quest, the Absolute.

Why can't sex just be sex? Pleasure and affection? Isn't it only our culture that wants sex to be the Answer?

Hey, wait a minute. Surely you do think it's the Answer, don't you?

What's the question?

The question? I don't get it.

You know, we've been hunting and whoring all these years looking for the Answer, and we don't even know what the question is. Isn't part of our addiction putting the cart before the horse?

When I was acting out, my beliefs never coincided with my actions. I knew what I was doing was wrong, but I could never bring myself to admit it.

I had moral standards, of course, but they always applied to other people. My addiction had turned me into a hypocrite.

A hypocrite. Double standard. Isolated. Divided.

That's what addiction does to you—it turns you against your own beliefs, against your own morality, against yourself.

Now, in recovery, I'm slowly putting the pieces back together again. It's like a jigsaw puzzle, and it's exciting trying to construct the final picture.

> *Yes, you were an old double talker. And of course, I didn't help, adding my angry voice to the dispute.*

At least you can admit that now.

> *That's true. And don't forget, I want to be part of the final picture, too.*

June 30
Patterns

I like to think that I'm free from the past, free as air, free just to be me.

> *Do you really believe that?*

Oh yes!

> *And what about history, family, childhood?*

History's bunk, you know that!

> *But if you're free, why aren't you happy?*

Well, I admit, there's a problem there. I do feel this weight, like a burden, kind of.

> *Your addiction?*

Yes, I guess. But, I mean, I get pleasure out of it, kind of.

> *That's the second "kind of."*

I know. You're smart. I'm miserable. I know there's a pattern, but I just won't look at it. Can you help?

> *Yes, and I will. Together we're changing the pattern. I do believe in history, but I also believe in change.*

But what about that mean old brutish voice of yours?

> *Oh, that? That's **past** history now!*

I work in a machine shop, and I have to be accurate and careful in everything I do. I like the work, but I get tense, especially as the week draws to an end.

I deserve to let go then and take a few risks. I used to ski a lot and do some sky-diving. But I wanted something stronger, you know, something where my inner life was involved.

When I started to act out sexually with prostitutes, I knew I'd found what I needed. I got high on the unknown, the risk, the deceit, the betrayal. My wife was kind of domineering anyway, and this was my secret revenge and my secret thrill.

Someone wrote her an anonymous letter. She put a private detective onto me. Divorced me. Got the kids. Took me to the cleaners for everything I'd worked so hard to build.

I've still got my secret life, but it's not the same now.

———————

Look, don't whine. You got exactly what you secretly wanted. And don't forget—you've still got the sex, anytime you want.

183

July 2
Castration

W hat's this castration business they're always talking about?

> *Difference.*

How's that?

> *Difference between the sexes and the generations.*

Mm. What else?

> *Not being One.*

Don't speak in riddles.

> *You want to be One, Unified, Omnipotent, the way you once longed to be.*

Why always me?

> *I mean, we all do . . . we want to be whole, self-sufficient, total, perfect. Just as we were in our childhood fantasy.*

And castration. . . ?

> *. . . is the mark of separation, maturation, difference. It means being sheared into individuality. Having a sex, a name, a place.*

Being just me, not the Ideal Me?

> *That's it. Just you. Cut off from Perfection—limited, partial, flawed, human. Can we live like that?*

We can try.

Even though I'm in a Twelve Step group and following the Program, I still slip now and again.

At first I beat up on myself, and all the voices from my past were shouting and screaming inside my head. It felt like a madhouse in there, in my mind.

But now if I have a slip, I'm able to keep a clear head and speak to myself calmly and kindly. I just don't give the the old voices time to start up their terrible cacophony.

I talk to a friend, admit what I've done, and then continue the conversation with myself in an adult manner.

I am replacing the old voices of slander and shaming with new voices of friendship and affection.

It makes a difference, believe me.

> *Yes, I can vouch for that. My voice was usually the loudest and the most shaming, but now I feel like a brother to you and not your angry father.*

That's good to hear.

> *That's good to know. And I mean it.*

July 4
Honestly

I think I'll just go and check out the soft-porn videos.

>*How come?*

Just to make sure I'm really cured.

>*Honestly?*

Well, sure. I mean, how can I tell if I'm really making progress unless I test myself now and again?

>*Are you being really honest with yourself? This isn't the first time, you know, that you've just been "checking things out."*

You're just talking that stuff from the group.

>*Why do you want to check things out?*

Well . . . I. . . . I know, it does sound a bit fishy now that I come to think about it.

>*Sounds very fishy to me. And I'm glad you're on to it, too.*

Thanks. I'm hearing something new in your voice. And it helps me keep things straight. Honestly.

>*You used to get so mad when we had these kinds of conversations. I'm really glad we can talk things over now. Honestly.*

There's something really sick about being addicted to sex . . .
but like all obsessions it has its funny side.

> *Tell me.*

Remember the time I'd just met Deborah, and my mother was
looking forward to seeing some snapshots of her during the
Christmas vacation?

> *Yes, and we were at college, and we packed everything
> up hurriedly at the end of the quarter and stuffed a lot
> of old papers into that black leather briefcase Mom
> gave us.*

And jumped into the old green Volvo and drove like crazy
along those New England roads.

> *Got home just in time to run upstairs and wash and
> change for dinner.*

Left the briefcase on the armchair at the end of the table.

> *And came down and found Mom spreading out a
> handful of pornographic photos along the edge of the
> dining-room table.*

And she was saying, "She looks charming, so young and
brown and strong, but I can't really see a thing. Do be a dear,
Charlie, and get my glasses!"

> *Of course, in those days you and I were always feuding
> and fighting, and I'm sure I made you feel like a guilty
> child. Thank heavens those days are over!*

July 6
Black cloud

Mom was always gloomy about something. Her teeth. Money. Job. Men. The world.

She loved me best. At least that's what she'd say. I was her "little lark," her "sunbeam," her "spark of life."

I felt bad for her. I really did. Especially when Dad left.

I thought: "She's had a rotten life. I've got to make it up to her. She's so sweet and alone."

I tried. I was still her "little sunbeam," but she was a black cloud. Always dark, always gloomy, always moaning.

There was no place for me, until boys came along—boys, and dope, and sex.

Lots of dope and sex.

Love?

No love.

That's too bad, little lark. Just remember, though. Mom didn't get into dope and sex. Don't blame her for everything. Heaven helps those who help themselves, you know.

I feel comfortable only when I'm alone, acting out with pornography.

> *Well, what's wrong with that?*

It seems such a lonely way to enjoy sex.

> *Yes, and you don't even seem to enjoy it much.*

That's true, but it's familiar and it isn't threatening.

> *For a while. But is it really comfortable in a positive sense?*

Well, I can see what you're saying; "comfortable" is a funny word.

> *I like the word, but not for pornography. Why not get really comfortable with yourself?*

Yes. It is a good word—in the right context. Thanks.

> *Good heavens! Do you remember the old days when this kind of talk would end in yelling and screaming? We've come a long way since then.*

Yes. I'm even beginning to feel comfortable with you.

July 8
Systems

Today is the second day without nicotine, after twenty a day for twenty years. The tempo of my life has changed completely: it's as if I were a horse, straining at the bit, wrenching at the bridle of my decision, hour after hour.

It's the same with my sexual acting out. The willful colt in me pulls and tugs and tries to wrench itself free from restraint. Mind and body struggle for the sick thrill that brings release and shame.

The voice of reason and the middle way seem so insignificant, at times, in the face of this raging addiction.

I need other voices and the clasp of friendship and support.

I accept my powerlessness, but I refuse to yield to the compulsion of my addiction.

I'm changing systems, painfully.

Yes, I know it is painful. How easy it would be to slide with a sigh back into the slough of our addiction! Change means pain, and it's hard. But it's worth it to be healthy again.

I remember how I persisted in acting out, even when there was no pleasure involved. Once the ritual began, nothing could stop me until the release of orgasm.

And then the shame that lay hidden just beneath the surface flared up and overwhelmed me. I'd run off as if pursued by the hounds of heaven.

I needed to wake up, to be brought to my senses. A therapist recommended a Twelve Step Program.

I was scared to share my squalid secrets with strangers. But after a while, inspired by the courage of the others, I came to speak about the exact nature of my affliction. People listened with compassion and love.

My burden of shame and loneliness gradually fell away from my shoulders.

I was back in the human community.

Of course I fought you all the way and called you a baby, a coward, a fool. I was crazy, too, you know, crazy with bullying anger. But you resisted and got free, and now there's a growing harmony between us.

July 10
Mourning

I feel as though I was cheated out of my childhood.

> *Yes, I know. That's true and it's hard.*

I mean, sex is complicated enough without that violence. Those attacks! It really poisoned my life as a kid. I want to forget it, but I can't, I can't.

> *Maybe we have to do some mourning first.*

Mourning? How can I mourn what I never had?

> *I think it's possible to grieve for something missing.*

But I don't miss it!

> *I mean the childhood that we should have had. The playfulness and the quick changes of mood, the zest for life and the hope.*

Especially the hope. I **am** starting to feel hope now, thanks to the Program.

> *The child in us is still alive and getting healthier every day.*

I wish we had known happier days.

> *If we talk about this enough, the pain will gradually diminish. And then the child will come alive again!*

I remember my first sexual high. I felt, "This is great! At last I've found something that is entirely mine."

And I sought that feeling again and again, setting everything up so that the pattern and the feeling kept on repeating themselves. Just for me.

But the more I acted out, the less pleasure I got; and gradually I found only remorse and disgust.

Now, in my program, I am getting in touch with real feelings that have to do with other people and relationships. Love, for example.

Love is a feeling that expands and endures.

You are changing every day.

You, too. Love is contagious, isn't it?

July 12
Confusion

Half the time my inner life was like a seesaw, lurching up
and down from euphoria to despair. Lust and disgust struggled
inside me.

I couldn't concentrate on my work, on my children, on my
friends, on the world outside me. It was like living in a
whirlwind, with no center.

And voices from the past made things worse, chiding me and
criticizing, always keeping me at a distance from myself.

I did the Fourth Step and made "a fearless moral inventory" of
myself. My sponsor worked with me and helped me set down
the good points as well as the bad.

I got some clarity and sanity and a new perspective on myself.
I felt balanced and stronger and more peaceful.

The Steps restore us to our true selves.

> *Yes, I have to admit you're right. I fought you all the
> way and made things as tough as I could, but you and
> the program won through. Maybe we'll find serenity
> together.*

Maybe?

> *We will find serenity together.*

I know I need to write some things down. I'm doing the Fourth Step and I need to make a list, take inventory, find things out.

> *Okay. That's a vital step.*

Yes, but I keep putting it off.

> *How come?*

Part of me thinks it's a waste of time, really. I mean, we live in the present, right? Who wants to go digging into all that murk and filth? Who needs it?

> *You do. We all do. If we don't try to understand our past—celebrate its beauty, fill in the gaps, bury the dead—it goes on affecting us, driving us like a hidden engine.*

Let the dead bury the dead. Dad's dead. I want to live!

> *But don't you think we all need to grieve and to mourn as well as celebrate and dance for joy?*

What? Wait. I think I see what you mean. We have to know what happened in order to move forward. Shedding old skins and beginning anew. And being sorry, without getting stuck back there?

> *Yes, that's it. It's taken me a long time to figure out that we don't have to keep the angry parent inside us just because Dad is dead. I understand Dad better now, and I don't believe he'd want me to be a bully and a tyrant.*

July 14
Changing places

You know, I didn't have to take Dad's place. I always had it.

Right from the first, she preferred me. She liked it when he was away. I know she did. She told me. She'd come and sit and watch me take a bath.

I knew what she was staring at. It made me feel big and proud.

And scared.

I mean, I couldn't have . . . really . . . could I?

I didn't really want to . . . you know. But then again . . .

She wanted to. And she wanted me to. I could tell.

I loved that feeling. It was like magic, later, with other women. It made me feel I could have anyone, anytime I wanted.

But then . . . it's a funny thing. I couldn't . . .

I wanted to, all the time.

But I couldn't.

I think you are really disgusting to talk like that about Mom. You get that filth from those magazines you're always reading. Just admit it, you're a pervert, that's all.

You know, ever since I've been in therapy and talked about my past, I'm coming to realize two things.

> *Speak, O sage.*

You're supposed to be the sage, wise guy. But anyway, two things—"It's not my fault," and "I'll always be that way."

> *That must make you feel comfortable.*

Comfortable?

> *Sure. You don't have to do anything about it because you can't. "Once an addict, always an addict."*

But I wasn't always an addict—you know that.

> *Sure, I know that. And that means "you can return to sanity," as we say in our group.*

Return?

> *Return.*

Do you really think so?

> *Do you?*

Well, I'm not sure, but . . . why don't we give it a try?

> *Together we can do a lot, you know. In the old days our house was divided against itself, and I couldn't stand that! We've taken off in a new direction! This way, not "that way."*

July 16
Euphoria

For sex addicts, euphoria seems like a state of permanent ecstasy. They strive to get out of themselves and fly beyond the boundaries of everyday reality.

I used to suffer from this delusion, and whenever the going got rough, I had to have my high, regardless of what it involved.

And often it involved not me or my partner, because we were both in love with the illusion and not the reality of sex.

Actually, euphoria means "well-being," and that is exactly what sex addiction is not.

It's good to be in recovery, to be well, to have found my own well-being.

> *How you loved your trips, whatever the cost! And we'd come home and then I'd have my turn, making you pay for all your artificial paradises.*

Yes, you were a brute . . . but I guess I deserved it.

> *It's different now, because you are getting in touch with the reality of your sexual desires.*

Whatever I do, I always feel there's something not quite right, something missing.

You mean you're missing something you once had?

No, I don't think it's that. I think it's always been missing.

How do you know, if you don't know what it is?

I see your point. But it's like . . . you know, you go out for a walk and the sun is shining and the air feels clean . . . and yet there's a shadow 'round the day, a shiver of gloom. There's nothing missing, but it's not perfect.

Do you want to be perfect?

How did you know?

Perfect, just like Dad?

Of course! You should know; you took over from Dad, and you're the one who's always telling me to be perfect.

Not anymore.

How come?

Because I really like you as you are.

Really? That is nice to hear. You're not so bad yourself, you know.

I think we're going to get along much better . . . now we know we're human.

July 18
Shaming

Every time a parent tells us who we are, we lose our sense of self and take on a mask, a persona. We let others define us.

Often that mask won't stand up to scrutiny, and so we feel unworthy and shameful.

From shame we turn to addiction as a place where we think we can be ourselves. Since we're not worth much, at least we can have that, our precious addiction.

And so the spiral continues: we act out, get caught, are shamed again, feel hopeless, run to our addiction.

One day we have to stop running.

> *When you were in shame, how easy it was for me to*
> *hurt you! And the more I yelled at you, the deeper went*
> *the shame. Just like the family all over again.*

I'm glad you're speaking in the past tense. Things are changing now.

> *Changing for both of us.*

Changing for the better.

In my sex addiction, I looked only at bodies, never whole people. I could only "have sex," because I was afraid of loving and being loved.

Love asks us to look beyond picture and surface, and I was terrified that I would find in deep feelings only the image of my own emptiness.

Now I am learning to talk to the people in my group and to relate to them in a nonsexual way.

This was so new that I was scared at first. But I am much more confident of what I am myself, as I get to know others and welcome difference.

I had to learn that it is difference and diversity as well as love that make the world go 'round.

> *Yes, I knew you were frightened and lonely—in part because I was always so hard on you. I took on Dad's role, and that messed us both up.*

You're right. It helps me to hear you acknowledge that. I'm not as scared of you as I used to be.

July 20
Love affair

I feel like having an affair.

> *Oh no, not again. Please!*

Why not? It's about time.

> *It's only been six weeks since you joined the group, and I thought one of your temporary boundaries was "no more affairs until I'm better."*

Well, I am better.

> *You can't be cured in six weeks. Come on now!*

Can't you see and feel the difference?

> *Well, it's true you are more lively and at the same time more relaxed. It is pretty amazing. What's happening?*

That's what I'm trying to tell you. I'm having this affair.

> *With whom?*

With life!

> *Well, you fooled me! I'm glad you've got your sense of humor back as well.*

Someone told me recently that the word incest means "joined" or "uncut"; and that gave me a jolt, I can tell you.

I've never really cut the cord and detached from my mother. It sounds crazy I know, but at forty, I'm still "mama's boy," playing at being Lover Boy.

That hurts, just to say it. But at the same time it's a relief to put it into words.

Words can't heal but they can begin the healing process. And naming helps. "I'm an incest victim."

There, that sounds grim and a bit crazy, but it's true and it's out there and I feel it's the beginning of a new adventure—the adventure of learning to break free and be me.

> *Wow, heavy stuff, man. Don't you feel you're betraying Mama, talking like that, out loud?*

You're joking, of course.

> *Of course.*

July 22
Powerlessness

How can I recover from my addiction if I have to **begin** by admitting I'm powerless?

> *Well, how powerful were you?*

How do you mean?

> *Over your addiction.*

Not very powerful.

> *And over your shame?*

Not at all.

> *You were in a losing system.*

Which system?

> *The shame-and-addiction system. It's a one-hundred-percent-guaranteed no-win system.*

Yes, that's true. I feel that. And now?

> *A new system. The hope-and-recovery system.*

How does that work?

> *You work, and the group works . . . together. You'll find support and love and a new system of power relations. If you want to.*

I do. Yes. Tell me, how do you know all these things?

> *I think you know them, too, deep down. It's just that your addict's voice sometimes drowns out the voices of reason and recovery.*

I used to keep a notebook and record my sexual triumphs. At night, I read the book and recited the names of my partners like a war song.

I didn't realize that this ritual only proved my fear, as well as my immaturity. I was trying to prove I was a man while forgetting to be human.

Friends in my program helped me see how destructive my behavior was. I learned to talk about my sexual fears and to overcome them.

Now I've stopped treating other people like victims, and I've learned that the most important triumph is to be open and honest and human.

> *You **were** a pain to be with—all that mirror stuff and the games and the keeping score. And I made you pay for it in a hundred ways.*

Yes, you did. And how you loved your power over me!

> *You gave it to me. But not anymore.*

No. Not anymore.

July 24
Icons

They say that it's love that makes the difference, and that's true.

But it's also difference that makes love—makes us love each other.

When I was in my addiction, I was afraid of difference—difference of sex, difference of age, difference of personality. I wanted to love all right, but I wanted to love someone just like me.

Now, in recovery, I can see that I was in love not with people but with icons. I created images that were like twin brothers or sisters of what I wanted to be. And I got angry because they were me—and yet not me.

I became violent and tried to destroy those icons which reminded me of how imperfect I am.

Now, in celebrating difference, I accept imperfection. I'm trying to learn to live as I am, and love what is human.

———————

That's really healthy, and it helps me, too.

Bravado

*Y*ou always seem so cool, so elegant these days. Is something wrong?

Who do you think you are, my therapist?

> *It's just that when you're **really** cool and self-assured and charming—the way you have been these past few days—it always means you're hiding something.*

Always? Why do you always say always?

> *Sorry. But why so aloof, so distant?*

I have to survive.

> *What a horrible expression! Survive. We have to live! Live!*

How can I live when . . .

> *Yes . . .*

. . . I'm covered in shame, like a snake?

> *Snakes can shed their skins, you know. Why don't we talk about this shame and go beneath it and beyond it?*

All right, let's try. I'm tired of being an old snake in an old skin.

> *Great! Maybe this is it, the breakthrough, the new beginning!*

Pollyanna!

> *I know. But it's exciting, isn't it?*

I suppose it is. Yes. Yes, it is.

July 26
Charming

As a liberated man, I like talking about my feelings. Women respond to men who are outgoing, sensitive, and caring.

I like to tell my story first—the unforgiving dad, the competitive brother, the hard times at school, California, the Liberation Therapy, my cozy men's group, some healthy crying, and now feelings, feelings, feelings.

I watch the effect, and then I calculate my responses to **her** story. I lean forward, look encouraging, and usually, at the end, put my hand over hers in a tender, caring way.

If she leaves her hand there, I know I'm on the way to another conquest. If she takes her hand away, I sometimes persevere with some talk about empathy and astrological signs; but usually I simply pay the check and leave. That doesn't happen very often, I can tell you.

This men's liberation thing really works.

> *You know, you're addicted to your own charm and blind to the reality of other people. You're simply prostituting yourself and your own values.*

Values? Values don't get you anywhere in this world.

> *You're going to be lonely. You are lonely.*

I'm fine as I am. Leave me alone.

July 27
Being happy

As a sex addict, I used to think that being happy was getting high on sex.

When that didn't happen, I'd get mad. And act out. And get mad.

And on and on.

I was looking for happiness instead of seeing it as a gift, a by-product of something else—affection, children, looking, walking, sailing, caring, working.

Now I can see that you can't look happiness in the face anymore than you can stare at the sun.

Since then, I've found real happiness in a hundred moments—often when I was least expecting it.

Being sane and sober takes the tension out of my life and lets me relish the moments of happiness as they come by, unannounced.

That's real progress, I must say. And I can share those moments with you now. I'm changing, too, thank heavens.

July 28
Nice guy

Joe is calm and quiet and cautious and respectful and considerate and gentle—the perfect husband . . . **and I could kill him!**

>*Steady. What happened?*

Nothing. Nothing happened. Nothing has happened for the three years since I met him. Nothing happened before I married him, during the marriage ceremony, or since.

>*Not much spice, eh?*

Spice! A sniff of pepper would blast him into orbit.

>*Why don't you buy. . . ?*

Thanks, I've read Ann Landers and I've got the black French hose, and the Taiwan panties, and the Kyoto *kamino*. But no bambino.

>*Kimono.*

I don't care what it's called. It doesn't work! Nothing works. Not even his awful magazines.

>*Hush, dear.*

Now you're sounding like him. I need helping, not hushing!

>*Right. Phone him and tell him. Then tonight sit down and talk to him. Be straight and strong. He needs help. He's got to get it. And make that a condition for your staying.*

P art of my addiction is mixing sex with other feelings.

Of course, I know there's never **just** sex.

But part of my problem is wanting to have sex when I'm angry. And then that makes me mad. And then I need more sex. And on and on.

I thought the main thing I had to do was to work on my addiction. But I'm learning that I need to work on anger and on the relationship between anger and sex.

I guess I get angry because I can't control things.

I can't control sex.

Sex, even good, healthy sex, has a life of its own. And that scares me and makes me mad.

So behind the anger is the desire to control. And behind that? Sex.

And behind that?

------

*You sound confused. Look, we can never know everything—and that's not the point, to **know** everything. But it's really good that we're working on the connection between feelings and sex. That certainly helps to get things straight.*

July 30
Desertion

I used to set myself up in one relationship after another to be left, abandoned. I hated it with all my soul, but I set it up.

It was a compulsion. I hated and feared it but I wanted it in some dark corner of my soul.

Being deserted, after all, was what I was used to. My dad left us when I was five and then I was sent off to a posh girl's school while my younger sister stayed at home and got all the love and warmth and treats.

I wanted to love and all I got was desertion, and that formed a kind of sick equation inside me: love and you'll get kicked in the teeth.

So I'd beat them to it; I knew it was coming anyway, so I'd get in there first and put on my martyr look and say, "I told you so." With a little shiver of pleasure.

I don't need that shiver anymore. In my group, I know people will be back every week, come hell or high water.

And I'm back, too, back to a secure self at last.

Well, I could be nasty and say, "it's taken you a while." You see, I still have a little bit of that mean streak in me. But seriously, I'm glad for both of us, glad you decided to heal yourself and come back home to you.

I think of the people with whom I used to have anonymous sex in the park, not as people, but as accomplices—not true partners, but partners in crime. A crime against the life I want to lead now.

> *You're right. They're criminals, and you are, too. And that's all you're fit for!*

Hey, wait a minute, there. Not so fast. I said "the people with whom I **used** to have anonymous sex."

> *Once an addict, always an addict. You'll see.*

I feel sorry for you, sometimes. That tired old voice of yours—it sounds like a broken record.

> *Well, someone's got to tell the truth.*

But it's not the truth, and you know it. I stopped that crazy behavior six months ago, and I'm beginning to feel fine about my recovery.

> *It won't last.*

Yes it will. And you know what? When you speak like that, you're an accomplice, too, an accomplice in the old life. Why not accept that we're changing, and work on our new relationship?

> *Well, you do sound healthy. Maybe we could give it a try. But I'm not exactly optimistic, you know. I've heard it all before.*

Wait and see, Wise Old Bird. And then you'll be the first to join in the celebration!

August 1
Hunt

Men say women are passive, but they don't know me.

If I have the hots for a guy, I spend every ounce of energy I have to get him where I want him. I bet I've got eighty percent of them, minimum, into my soft little bed ever since I was first sexually active, oh, many moons ago.

I'm not really interested in sex **per se**, you understand. In fact, between you and me and the bedpost, I've never actually had an orgasm. I can moan and groan with the best of them, though, and men are so dumb they'll swallow anything.

No, it's not the sex I like, it's the hunt.

I work in a large corporation and I go to all the functions. If I meet a guy I like the look of, I find out all I can about him, then I hang around, smiling, looking coy, brazen, ready, dependent. Men are so dumb that they end up thinking they've made all the moves, when all they've done is pick up the tabs.

There's only one thing. I think about it all day, from morning to night. I can't get anything done. And I can't sleep sometimes, either.

It's not the sex, you understand. Just the hunt.

I think I understand. I need to learn more about this so I can help instead of criticizing all the time. I hear what you say and I think it's time we went and talked to someone about this, don't you? Not another guy, no, a professional, a therapist. We need help.

A child who loses touch with a parent or a loved one feels bereft and abandoned. Love is stifled. Love is lost.

So we turn away and seek affection in the illusion that sex is the same as love.

Each time I began to feel lost or deserted, the same mechanism clicked into gear: sex for solace, sex for contact, sex at any price.

And then I started to pay the price. I found I couldn't do without sex, and yet sex didn't yield any returns. Sex itself became abandonment.

I had to live that torment before I could take the First Step and find a new sense of affection and trust.

> *We both knew what was going on and yet we were at war with each other and couldn't change. Only now, as we work the Program, are we learning to live together.*

There's still some friction between us from the old days, you know.

> *Yes. But as we confront it, the abrasiveness wears itself out.*

August 3
Double bind

My mother never raised her voice and yet I felt she was always angry. The fact is, she **was** angry but afraid to admit it. At the same time, she let me see that she really wanted to be angry, deep down. She was a crook.

My mother would promise to take me to the park and then she'd forget, or deny that she had promised. She was a liar.

My mother would ask me how I felt and then tell me all about her aches and pains. She was selfish.

My mother would say I looked pretty . . . but she was looking at my sister.

It seems crazy to be saying these things at my age, but I need to talk myself into some traps my mother set for me.

And then talk my way out again.

> *Yes, that's very healthy. And don't forget that, for years, I took over your mother's voice and kept the double binds alive. You can hate me for it, if you like . . . but remember, nice girls don't hate their mothers! Seriously, if you hate me, you're also hating yourself.*

I know. I'm working on that, too.

Addicts are adept at denial. We have the strange power to look ourselves in the eye and say, "I'm not sick; I'm just having fun. No problem."

But fun is precisely what we don't have. It's hard, miserable work being a sex addict and denying it too.

Addiction takes its toll. I felt as if my whole life were one long trail of misery until I was forced by my despair to break out of denial and start to change my life.

Denial is what keeps the addiction alive; it's the engine that helps to drive the disease.

When we break free of denial we are truly on the road to recovery.

> *I used to love to hear your excuses and defiance and refusal to face the facts. Then I knew I had you! It's different now; you've changed the rules and I've changed sides. I'm with you now. That Program really works, brother!*

Yes. It works. For both of us. For all of us.

August 5
Blinders

You remember those old horses you used to see pulling carts through the streets in New York? They wore those weird blinders, those leather things on the sides of their eyes so they wouldn't look around and see the sights.

> *Yes. I remember. Blinders.*

That's it. That's what I said.

> *You said "blinkers."*

Well, what's the difference?

> *They're different words, that's all. That makes the difference. Let's not be sloppy about language.*

Let's not be so pedantic about language. You made me forget what I wanted to say. Oh, yes. It was about my addiction.

> *It's like blinders?*

Blinkers. Yes, that's it. When I'm in my addiction, I don't see the world, I don't look up and look around, I don't love and live, because of my addiction, my blinkers.

> *Blinders. But yes, I know what you mean, and you're right!*

Many sex addicts like to test themselves: they embark on their rituals "just to see what happens."

We think we can control our actions, but once the ritual is set in motion, it always takes over, as if it had a life of its own.

I used to play that game, driving along the same street, stopping at the same intersection, checking out the same scene, "just to see what would happen."

Of course, I always acted out, powerless once I had passed the point of no return.

Now, in my program, I don't feel I have to test myself or engage in any ritual. The Program is the structure within which I take the steps towards sanity.

The only testing I do now is checking the progress of my recovery.

You really have changed, I can feel it.

And what about you, Superdad?

Me? I've always been perfect, of course.

A perfect tyrant, I'd say! But now you're changing, too.

August 7
Discord

You seem kind of edgy, today. Want to act out?

I don't want to, but I will, I feel it. I'll be on the way home
and then just a little swerve and a quickie with Dolly.

> *Dolly's a good name. You treat her like a little baby, a
> little plaything.*

That's what I want, you know that. And I love her baby voice.

> *That's fine with me. You're just a little boy, so why not
> have your little fun with your little dolly?*

Always belittling, always sneering.

> *Well, what do you expect, little baby, Mama's baby.*

Just what we've got, the two of us. Hatred and strife. That's
how we set it up. What else do you expect, you vicious sadist?

> *Nothing.*

Same here. Nothing.

> *Hey! Time out! We'll never get anywhere if we go on
> like this. I want us to help each other, change the rules,
> make a truce, join a group—anything to get away from
> this warfare.*

Not a hope.

When I marry him, I'll fix him.

I know he likes those sexy magazines and porno shops, but I'll change all that.

He's sweet, like a little boy. I know he's got a lot of hurt and anger in him, but I'll soon soothe that.

He was violent once, out of the blue. Slapped me. Sent me hurtling across the room. I can deal with that. And anyway, he didn't mean it.

He likes to drink with the boys, and sometimes he comes home drunk. He flies off the handle if he doesn't get his own way. And he always fixes himself a drink before we make love.

He admits he drinks too much.

He's promised to change and I know he can.

And anyway, I can make it work out for both of us.

> *You give yourself so much power! Tell me—what are you really afraid of? You're fooling yourself if you get married talking and thinking like that. Please listen to me. You know you can trust me now, don't you?*

I don't know what you're talking about.

August 9
Slippery

When we fall back into our addiction, we say we've had a slip. And if we are wise, we feel sorry, make amends, and move on.

Sex addiction is a slippery customer; it comes to us on the sly, in a covert, clandestine way. Before we know it, we are acting out, like zombies.

To be free of it, we need to be vigilant and gentle and follow our program.

But if we do slip, we don't have to beat ourselves up and go back down into the pit of despair. We can admit we've had a moment of powerlessness and then take heart from our program and our group.

Take heart, feel hope, move on.

> *Yes, that makes sense. You didn't talk like that in the old days. I'm glad to hear the new strength in your voice and courage in your heart.*

Do I sound a bit preachy?

> *A bit. But better that than the old lies and excuses, don't you think?*

I think my dad wanted to love me, but he was always putting me down in little ways.

"Not for you." "Not for girls." "Peter will do it." "You can't manage that, darling." "Be a lady."

Those words still go 'round in my head, even now. Especially when I want to try something new, I keep hearing these sentences that have hardened into slogans.

Even in my group I hear them. And it bothers me that I have to admit my powerlessness when I keep hearing these voices that sap my confidence. What I need is more power, not less.

Perhaps these groups are just for men, like most everything else in our culture.

Where do I belong?

> *I hear you, and these are real concerns. The group isn't the whole answer, though. What we find there is a new sense of community and a new system in which addiction loses its grip on us. And that's happening, don't you think?*

Yes. And I do feel stronger every time I go.

> *We go.*

Thank you. Yes. Every time we go.

August 11
Sex objects

Why did I always treat people as sex objects?

>*Yes, why did you?*

I refused to see the otherness and difference in people; I only wanted to find the same things in them that gave pleasure to me.

>*Like a shadow?*

You mean, the other person was like a shadow of me—an extension, not a person?

>*Yes. A shadow or an ideal image.*

But I debased them. I didn't idealize them.

>*Right. You debased them because you made them into images, not people. The images were what you wanted, and you idealized them.*

Yes, I see. Ideal images, unreal people.

>*That's it. What made you change?*

The group. When I heard different stories, I realized that other people exist as free and living people. I wanted to know these people as human beings.

>*Living human beings and not dead sex objects.*

That's exactly right.

>*You know, part of the problem was that we treated each other like objects, you and I—always criticizing and demeaning each other. We can do better, don't you think?*

Yes I do. Thanks for your insights; they help a lot.

I feel her like a knife in my side.

Wherever I go, whether I open or close my eyes, I see her, dancing in front of me.

In the bright sun, I stagger and almost fall. She is there, dancing, just out of reach.

I feel faint. I need help.

It's so hot. I go into a church and pray that she will be torn out of me like a piece of my flesh.

I think I will die. I remember the old poets and their eternal theme, Love and Death. I can't even smile at the irony of it all . . . at my age, a critic, wise and detached, in love with a woman—no, a girl—no, a line of verse, a phantom, nothing really, nothing.

Except it is devouring my life.

———————————

You asked for it, wasting your life away in those dusty old books. And now that a slip of a girl reads you a couple of her poems and takes you to her couch, you fall apart like a ruined building. Folly, sheer folly, and comic, too, from my perspective.

August 13
Self-absorbed

I used to have to make an effort to listen to other people; I was so busy wondering about their bodies and their sex lives. Maybe we could get together sometime, maybe tonight, maybe after lunch. . . .

Of course it was my own pleasure I wanted, my own thrills, my own orgasm, my own high.

My body was my ego and I was in love with it.

In my Twelve Step Program I'm learning to listen to others and imagine their pain and their joy as they recover. Other lives have become important to me; I relate to new friends in recovery.

It's taken an effort to detach from myself and empathize with others.

But it's worth it: I'm slowly clambering out of my selfish little world.

> *Yes, you were in love with yourself, but at the same time you hated yourself.*

And you hated me, too, and increased my self-hatred. Don't sound so aloof and superior!

> *You're right. We were at war, and I was hateful.*

Peace. Let's work together for peace.

No one starts life as a sex addict. Neglect, abuse, perfectionism, unclear boundaries—some trigger has to be there to start the disease in motion.

Sex addiction is a response, a reaction to outside stimuli. We find escape from pain or release from tension in a sexual scenario and then we get hooked.

And our lives are half-lives lived in the gloom of self-absorption and lust.

I understood what life could really be like only when I started my recovery. Now I feel full of promise and hope.

It's like waking up to a world full of light.

> Yes, we did love the secrecy and the darkness, you and I. Just the two of us, locked in our private strife, isolated and lonely. And we were our own worst enemies.

I know. Just like the family all over again.

> Yes. But we can change.

Change and get well.

August 15
Making amends

Part of the Twelve Step Program is the willingness to make amends to those we have harmed through our addiction.

We don't have to write to the newspapers or go on TV or even make the rounds of every single person we have harmed.

I started by feeling sorry and admitting to myself and my Higher Power the harm I had done. I worked on my primary relationships and won back a feeling of self-respect and affection for others.

Then I was free to choose how to make amends.

How I go about it is my business—part of the active business of healing.

> *That's it. You don't have to be reborn a saint, you know. That was part of your problem, wanting to be perfect.*

I know. But your voice was always ready to chide me if I fell away from the Perfect Path.

> *That's true. I was Mom and Dad and God, all in one!*

If we can just be human, that's challenge enough.

 W hat's wrong? You've been so subdued lately.

> *I know. I feel lousy. The healthier you get, the sicker I feel!*

Well, in a weird way I miss your bullying voice, even though I hated it.

> *Don't you think you deserve it?*

No. Yes. I used to. But that's all over, isn't it?

> *Is it? What's happening now? I can't stand it. You're changing.*

It's the group, and the Program, and the readings, and my sponsor, and the phone calls, and the meetings, everything! It's wonderful what's happening. Haven't you noticed?

> *Yes. And it makes me sick that you, an intellectual, could swallow all that mystical stuff about surrender and group consciousness and Higher Power.*

I see. That's it. You're jealous! But the point is, it's not mystical sentimentality and swooning. It's solid, practical, down-to-earth, loving, grown-up talking, support, strength, and loving.

> *That's twice you said "loving."*

Loving. Loving. Just so. That's what it's all about.

> *It really has affected you. You look well, eat well, work well. If only you could talk well, the way you used to. All this "loving" stuff, I just can't relate to it. I'll keep listening and maybe I'll get to understand. But I doubt it.*

August 17
Lying

I used to look at myself in the mirror and feel shame in my own eyes. I knew that my life was being blasted by the secrecy and lying caused by my sex addiction.

When I was away from my wife I would spend hours fantasizing about other women, and when I couldn't find someone to have sex with, I would go into porno shops and find another man to masturbate me.

I lived a life of panic and emptiness. Nothing was true and real except my acting out and my shame and disgust.

As a sex addict, I was lost in a labyrinth of deceit and deception. The cure is honesty and openness. I want to be able to look myself in the eye with pride.

---

*You know, you used to **enjoy** lying, in some perverse way. And I encouraged your lies so I could be mean to you. We were at odds with the world and ourselves. I'm glad we're learning to be friends.*

You know, I hate talking about this—but about those bathhouses I used to go to.

   Yes. I remember.

I never found what I was looking for, did I?

   What were you looking for?

I'm not sure.

   But you know you never found it?

Yes. This sounds crazy, but I think I was looking for the right thing, but in the wrong place.

   So what were you looking for?

Promise you won't laugh?

   I promise.

I trust you now, you know.

   I'm glad. And now, that thing you were looking for and didn't find, because you were looking in the wrong place . . . let's not forget that.

No, let's not.

   What was it then?

Love.

   I'm glad you can say that now and say it loud and clear. And you know, it doesn't sound crazy at all, does it?

August 19
Controlling

Many sex addicts feel that they are helpless to control their lives. So sex becomes a way of seeking to achieve power.

When we masturbate, we have the illusion of being in control; there is nobody to interrupt our fantasies and our actions, nobody to threaten us with criticism or demands or even responses.

Often masturbation becomes the only safe sex, the only controlled activity for the addict, who fears being taken over by others.

In my recovery, I've learned that other people don't always want to trespass on my freedom or control my life. They are content to let me be.

Now I can take the risk of a sexual relationship with someone other than myself. And I'm still here and still free.

> *Yes, I know you thought you'd lose your identity in a sexual relationship with someone else. But when you discovered the power of love, you could take the risk of reaching out.*

I'm glad we're **both** giving up control and finding power.

Like many girls, I grew up with the idea that marriage is the only way to be fulfilled.

One day when I was about thirteen, I was playing in the barn with my cousin Lisa. She was lying in the hay with the evening sun slanting across her body like gold. I jumped on her and started kissing her like a demon.

She screamed and ran and told Mom. She and Dad kind of made light of it, but Lisa's Mom was really angry.

Lisa didn't come around anymore.

My parents never sat down and talked to me about my feelings. They let me bury them.

So I buried them—my parents and my feelings. I swore nobody would ever make me feel weird and vulnerable again.

And I've kept my word.

The only snag is I feel crazy a lot of the time, crazy and empty.

It serves you right. You know what your real feelings are . . . they're perverted and unnatural. No wonder you're lonely. You're an outcast.

August 21
Split

Of course I love my wife, she's the One and Only for me.

But you need other women, too, all the time, don't you?

Yes, but that's not a threat. I need that, it's just for me.

Not a threat to whom?

To my wife, of course. She knows she's up there on the
pedestal and always will be. My beloved. My One and Only.

And in the meantime, sex as usual after lunch.

Look, it doesn't hurt anyone. And my wife has kind of given
up about sex.

*Are you sure? Aren't you scared of sex, except with
someone you don't respect?*

Maybe you're right. What if you **are** right? What can we do?

Talk about it, together.

Sounds good to me.

*Well that's a switch. It sure makes a change from
feuding and fighting. It's good to talk things over.*

And it's good to hear your kindly voice. I'm amazed at how
much your compassion helps me. I need to learn to listen.

When I first looked at a pornographic magazine, I knew they'd got it exactly right: there was my body for all the world to see, spread across the glossy pages in bits and pieces.

I felt my mother's breast come away from her body as I sucked at the milk that wasn't there. And she could magically get her revenge by biting me back and tearing out my nipple. An eye for an eye and a nipple for a nipple, that was how it was between Mother and me.

And then, of course, the penis came into the picture, hidden but threatening, driving me out and yet egging me on. I retaliated with my darkest, most lustful fantasies.

It was a world of whirling fragments, bits and pieces of bodies in orbit, before we all settled down into being real people, precariously.

I'm back in that earlier world when pornography sets me on edge. All those old lusts, and passions, and wars, and humiliation.

And retaliation. That's what they want, those men who plaster that stuff all over our culture.

Retaliation.

> *I can't make you out when you go off into that world of speculation. It's just sick, that stuff, and the more you try to analyze it, the sicker it seems. Isn't it enough to say pornography is filth and degradation . . . even though you must admit it is thrilling, isn't it?*

It's sick.

August 23
Seven deadly lies

I had a little list of lies I used to tell myself every time I wanted to act out in loveless encounters with men. I know they're just old cliches, but they always worked for me. I can still remember all of them.

"It doesn't hurt anyone."

"It feels good and it's just for me."

"I've worked so hard and I deserve some fun."

"I need to get rid of the tension."

"I need touching and holding."

"There's a lot of potential here, really."

"This is really all I deserve."

I guess the bottom line of all those little lies is . . . the bottom line: "That's all I deserve."

And that was all I thought I deserved. Why? Because I had no value, no idea what it was like to have a sense of worth and to care for myself as a creature of the world with a spark of the divine.

Thanks to my group and my Higher Power, I've torn up my list and substituted the Twelve Steps for the Seven Deadly Lies.

Don't get overconfident, now. You sound like a smoker who's been hypnotized into a two-week recovery. You can't just start your life from scratch, you know. There are still those old voices and tapes to remind you how worthless you were. And don't forget me! I'm still here, and here to stay.

We often say we're having fun when we're acting out, but really we know we're just acting. Beneath this mask of "fun" lie shame and fear.

I had to convince myself that the highs of my addiction meant I was having a good time, even though deep down I knew I was sick and lonely.

A voice would tell me, "Yes, why not do it? It will be fun. And you deserve some fun; we all do."

Finally I sank to the depths. I realized there was nothing amusing or satisfying about my life as a compulsive womanizer.

I came to admit that I needed a different way of relating to myself and others in the real world around me. At last the mask was off. The pure joy of living could begin.

I must admit you were obsessed by having fun, and you liked to brag about it. You were like a spoiled child, and I was the angry, scolding parent. No wonder we never got along! Now things are changing, day by day.

August 25
Pain

It hurts so much being lonely and outside.

> *But you're getting things together in the group and you have friends now.*

I know. You're right. But I'm still that scared and lonely child.

> *Yes, I feel it. And I used to punish the child in you. But now I don't, do I?*

No, not so much, that's true. But the pain's still there.

> *And that makes you want to act out, to try and medicate the pain?*

Yes. I run to sex from the pain. And find more pain. What can I do?

> *Phone someone up. Do your daily reading. And then let's take a walk.*

Yes. And talk. Let's keep on talking.

> *Yes. Our voices are different now. They go deep and can become springs of healing.*

One of the lovely aspects of recovery is seeing the world through fresh eyes.

I used to be so intent on getting my own pleasure that I rarely looked outward at things around me.

My fantasies absorbed me. They left me little time to observe and enjoy the world. I was blinded by my addiction.

Now I have more energy and more desire to turn outward toward the world. I am learning to look and listen and watch.

A cloud building up over a lake, a kitten at play, sunlight in my room, leaves floating under the bridge, a friend's painting—traces of life so beautiful in their particularity. How rich and splendid it all is!

---

*Well, you really **are** changing! We both are. Remember the times when we used to be thinking only of ourselves and the next fix? You're fun to be with now!*

August 27
Blame

I liked my older brother Andrew. He always gave me treats and told me stories.

I had a feeling he was lonely. Other people laughed at him behind his back.

One day we were sitting by the stream at the end of the garden. The air was heavy and moist. It was evening, and the crows were cawing in the trees.

He took my hand and put it on his penis. Together we rubbed his penis until he sighed and nodded. Then we both were silent.   It was like a dream.

I knew what had happened, and yet I didn't know, exactly. I felt afraid, and I felt sorry for my brother. He liked it. It was wrong. I needed to talk. He was silent. In that silence I felt an accusation.

All summer long we played that same game often. Once my brother cried. I wanted to tell Mom, but somehow I knew it was my fault, too.

When things get tough for me now, I still go off to the end of the garden.

Alone.

This is your secret, and you will carry it with you to the grave. You can't talk about this kind of stuff. Think of the family. Nobody would believe you anyway. It's sick. And sad. You're right. You're all alone.

Many people have said that life is like a journey and all of us are linked together as travelers on the road of life.

I used to feel solitary and unwanted. I felt that my life was a journey that nobody had ever taken before and nobody understood.

My sex addiction made me an outcast.

Gradually, in my Twelve Step Program I am learning that nothing I have done can place me outside the human community. People understand and care for me as a person, regardless of my past.

This came like a bolt from the blue. What! I am loved, needed? I am no longer alone and out in the cold? Heavens, what a joyful feeling!

Yes, I am back in the human community and on the path to health and sanity.

———————————

*Yes, it's true that you are loved. And now, don't say, "If only they knew!" People **do** know you, and they love you for who you are.*

August 29
Fears

I have to tell you something.

> *I'm here.*

Thanks. It's about happiness.

> *What about it?*

I'm scared of it. I like this guy and I want to be with him. . . .

> *What might happen?*

It won't last. You remember, as a kid, whenever I was fond of someone, she died, or one of my animals was run over. And then there was Dad.

> *How did he come into it?*

Well, I finally made up my mind to love him when I was about five. He turned me down.

> *Yes, I remember. That's when Sally was born.*

Right. So I decided: Okay, this Life business, I'm going to tough it out. And I'll never, never, never, never . . .

> *Make myself vulnerable, right?*

Never take a risk.

> *Never believe I deserve to be happy.*

Never trust. Never love. Never, never, never. That does sound kind of silly, come to think of it. Maybe just this once . . .

> *Great! Sometimes just getting things out in the open makes them less scary . . . and a little laughter doesn't hurt, either.*

Pornography was a drug for me. I used to look at my dad's secret collection and retreat into a world of silence and shame.

I knew, somehow, that what I was doing was harming me, and yet I needed to escape from the pain and anger I felt in a family of violence and abuse.

The pictures became my reality and everything else seemed frightening and unpredictable. With my pornography, I was in control.

Now in my group, I can talk openly about my addiction and even laugh about it a little. It doesn't have so much power over me anymore.

I am learning to sense the reality of other people without being afraid. And that helps me put the pornography where it belongs—in the garbage.

Yes, it does belong in the garbage. I'm glad we don't need to deal with that rubbish anymore.

August 31
Always

You know, I'm working hard in my group, but I'm not getting anywhere. I'll always be the same.

> *How do you know?*

Because that's what I've always felt about myself. I'm no good and I'll always be that way.

> *That makes things easy for you.*

How do you mean?

> *If you're always going to be the same, then there's no point in even trying to change.*

That's not what I meant. But I see your point.

> *The point is that often we resist change most when change is most powerfully taking place.*

Does that apply to me, by any chance?

> *What do you think?*

Yes, I think it does. I mean, in my heart of hearts I know I want to change, and I know that life is never static, and so why don't I learn to accept change . . . I want to accept it . . . really, I do accept it . . .

> *Look! You're changing even as you speak! And certainly, we've been changing, you and I, in the way we speak and listen to each other. Hey! We're going to make it.*

244

I used to give myself permission to act out.

I know that sounds crazy. But I'd say: "You've had a rough time today, you deserve a trip to the porno shop," or "Look, it doesn't hurt anyone to look at those movies, and anyway it gets rid of the tension."

I thought I was being good to myself by setting up some sex—it seemed to calm me down. But the snag was that it drove me away from my lover because I couldn't own my behavior.

I couldn't even look her in the eye. I wasn't there. I was lost in my images.

The road back from pornography hasn't been easy. But it's taken me back to a place where I really want to be. Reality.

———————————

You seem to be giving yourself permission to be a real person now. That's a healthy change, and it makes me feel good, too. We're in this together, you know.

September 2
A word from Dad

Of course I've always believed in progress—all good Americans do—but when I said progress, I thought "perfection."

That was Dad's idea, not mine. How can Dad's thought become my thought, when I didn't even believe it? It's weird: I mean, as a kid I was kind of mellow, always tinkering and fooling about, getting along okay, talking now and then about progress . . .

And thinking **perfection** (and shame). Dad's words.

I liked my body. I was good at sports and wanted to keep fit. I didn't smoke and never got into drugs. I was just a kid, taking it easy, hanging loose. Scared, of course, deep down.

And then one summer day, down by the edge of the cornfield, I had sex with Todd, my older brother.

Dynamite! A whole new world.

And now I really heard Dad's voice, loud and clear.

Perfection, and **shame.**

> *And then I took over.*

Yes. More perfection and still more shame.

> *Want to work on it?*

Yes. Instead of trying to be perfect, I want to try to understand and be human.

I hated it when my dad pretended to be my big brother and made sexual jokes. Half the time I didn't know what he was talking about, but of course I laughed and pretended to know it all.

It was always about boys, and petting, or "getting it on," or "having it off"—and always the little snigger and the wink.

I hated it, and so I hid my own sexuality like the plague. I never saw Dad and Mom being sexual or even playful with each other. They were like robots.

In a weird way, I thought Dad had his eye on me. He often seemed to come into my room just when I was putting on my bra or coming out of the bath. And always the little wink and the joke.

It was disgusting. I can't explain it. Nothing happened, but I felt dirty and defiled and ashamed.

I still do.

That's just because you're afraid of sex, you stupid little Puritan—but you think about it all the time. Dad was just trying to loosen you up and prepare you for the real world. But of course, you thought he was after your precious little body. You would!

September 4
Wilderness

Sex addiction takes us out of ourselves and plunges us deep into the thicket of shame and torment.

We struggle and wrestle with our desires, but we always end up acting out in restlessness and rage.

And then comes the loneliness, the self-hatred, the contempt.

And the voice inside us that slanders and punishes us, the voice that comes from long ago and far away but is as close and familiar as our addiction.

How I hated that voice, and yet how I loved my addiction! I was split and divided from my true self.

Thank God I've returned to sanity through my program and my newfound strength.

And I've found new voices of courage, affection, and hope.

Yes, I'm glad, too, that those crazy voices aren't still taking their toll. We can all change if we really want to and come back from the wilderness of sex addiction.

You know, I never really understood how people can talk from the gut. Does the gut even have a language?

Well, no, but you need to get in touch with your feelings.

That sounds like the party line. I hear that all the time in my group . . . but what about the mind and reason?

They are important, too. If we all just followed our feelings, we might be totally selfish and addicted.

So?

Feelings are important, but we need a framework and values within which to discuss them.

The Program?

Yes. That's why we don't just emote in the group; we discuss the Steps and the way to work them honestly and sanely.

I see. That helps, yes. It really helps. It's good to talk to you in a reasonable way.

Thanks. Do you remember how we used to sit around and shout at each other? Those certainly weren't the good old days.

September 6
Fantasy

I used to think I had a rich, imaginative life because I could invent all kinds of scenes of acting out.

Gradually these scenes started to be all the same. I kept on repeating them anyway, until I got sick and tired of viewing sex like a second-rate TV drama.

My fantasies were still-lifes, lacking any energy or vitality or uniqueness.

When I talked about these fantasies in my group, the fixed images began to dissolve. I'd even laugh at myself for being so compulsive and rigid. Gradually I began to feel free.

Free to invent, compose, imagine, change.

I remember those rigid fantasies that we repeated day after day, night after night. How silly it all seems now. It helps to laugh at our absurd obsessions.

One of my friends was in a group for sex addiction and I laughed when he talked about "sexual sobriety." I asked him if that meant he'd given up sucking at the bottle!

The joke was on me, really. I couldn't control my own sexuality, and I couldn't own up that I needed help.

One day this same friend asked me to come to his group "just to see."

I went and understood and stayed.

And now I own my own sexuality rather than being a victim of it. And I can choose to have sex or to abstain.

That's what we call sobriety—having a sense of proportion, a measure of influence over our own sexuality, a new tranquility.

I was totally out of control and now I'm my own person. And that's a sobering thought.

> *It took me a while to get used to this new voice—so confident and healthy. I'm glad you've come through.*

And what about you, Mr. Smug?

> *We've come through together.*

September 8
Showing off

I want to show myself to somebody.

> *Why? Do you feel sexual?*

No. Angry.

> *What do you want to do then?*

Be looked at, admired, I suppose.

> *And the anger?*

Well, if you want to know, I don't think people find me attractive, and I want to expose myself . . . I don't know . . . to get attention . . . and revenge, somehow.

> *Does it make you feel good?*

For a second, a flash. And then I feel humiliated and even more lonely.

> *Try and think beyond the flash, then. You'll probably find you don't really want to end up feeling hopeless and lonely. Think it through to the end. Think of the other people, too.*

Yes, I know. You're right. It doesn't make sense. I can do without it. Let's keep on talking.

> *Great! If we can get beyond the moment, the urge, I think we can stop this craziness. It sure feels good to talk instead of acting out.*

At first I could get high on the simplest sexual act. But as my addiction increased I had to find more and more exotic ways of getting my thrills.

All I wanted was sensation, excitement, release. And I wasn't hurting anyone, was I?

Except myself.

I became more and more obsessed, more and more frantic—until nothing would satisfy unless there was real danger and real pain.

Only when my life became totally unmanageable did I reach out for help and support.

It was touch and go. But I found a Twelve Step group that helped me heal my shame and turn to the world in love and not addiction.

> *It sure was touch and go! And of course, being the monster that I was, I kept the old voice of shame and hate alive.*

Yes. You encouraged my self-hatred and shame.

> *And you?*

I made it easy for you.

> *And now?*

Peace.

September 10
Saying it

Was it just an excuse, or was I really a victim?

What do you think?

I don't know. Sometimes I think I could be making all that stuff up.

The stuff about Dad?

Yes. Maybe he did really love me, like he kept on saying all the time.

All the time he was abusing you. First playing, then touching, then having sex with you.

Do you have to say it?

Yes. We both have to say it, and challenge it.

Challenge?

Yes. Challenge the stories he told you, the lies, and the deceit. Get clear of all that stuff. Move forward. Live!

Yes, I know you're right. It's just that it's hard . . . to remember that someone I love . . .

Go on. Say it. It's all right. Say it.

. . . someone I loved raped me.

We can come through, you know, if we work together.

Part of our addiction is the mechanism of denial. Because I couldn't face what I was doing, I turned away from myself and my actions. I buried myself in my addiction.

I denied I was out of control and in need of help. Nothing and nobody could get through to me.

One day I was arrested for acting out in a public place. I saw that my whole existence was a fraud and my life had become unmanageable.

I needed a new sense of power and a new sense of myself.

By joining a group, I accepted the fact that I needed help—and I surely have found it, in the love and support we give one another.

> *You had to learn the hard way, and I was always there, criticizing and shaming you. It's been a long road for us both, but we're going to come through, I know it.*

Are you sure?

> *Yes. Sure.*

September 12
Competition

I look in the mirror and I think, "Jean was looking really pretty last night, and I look like such a slob." Or, "Why can't I play tennis like John, I always seem to lose."

I'm a loser, a loser.

Is life a competition, then? The victory of the fittest and the prettiest and the smartest? How silly! That's just Dad's stuff, the old man's stuff.

I want to live my own life, at my own pace, with my own values, for me. If I can live like that, then I'll be good to myself and to others. And I'll learn to enjoy life and play—for the fun of it.

Life may be a game, but it's not a competition.

———————————

You're right. I know I've been trying to get you wound up with this competitive stuff. I've been playing Dad, playing God. Let's simmer down and enjoy life as we are.

People talk a lot about old Adam, but I think we should also talk about OME.

> *Good. Go on. What's OME?*

OME is Old Male Ego—being divided from your true self, obsessed with performing, being tough, masking feelings, having sex in the head, being scared, being scared to be scared, playing God, feeling worthless, trying to be perfect, not admitting you're wrong, not saying you're sorry, not crying, going it alone, competing, being grandiose, being programmed to be macho, choosing to be macho, being macho, killing the child within, splitting sex off, being a divided self.

> *Back to our beginnings. The old warfare.*

Yes, self-division in the guise of a perfect ego. But, really, the more we want to be a Perfect Whole, the more we end up being a perfect asshole!

> *That's a little blunt . . . but I see the point. And I should, because I was one of the irrational reasons for our self-division, wasn't I?*

Yes, and I was the other. Sounds as if we ought to get together on this.

> *Yes. And form the Perfect Whole!*

Oh no! No! No! No! Let's be content to be human.

September 14
Faith

When I became addicted to sex, I lost faith—in myself and in life.

In fact, maybe I became an addict **because** I lost faith.

I was married—to my childhood sweetheart. I really adored him and we were great together, especially in bed. In fact that's where it all started, in bed, all those years ago.

And then he dumped me for a woman ten years older. He didn't say a word . . . just packed up one weekend when I was at Mom's . . . packed up and left.

No note. Nothing.

I've no faith anymore, especially in sex. But I sleep around a lot, anyway.

I like to get men turned on.

And then I dump them.

That's the way to go. That's all they deserve. Pigs!
Pigs, the lot of them—just as Mom always said!

September 15
Voiceless

When I was a girl, I was really good at saying what they all
wanted to hear. In fact, I set up a little theater in my room and
lined up my dolls as an audience. "Yes, ma'am, you're right."
"It's just like you said, Dad." "I'll be there." "No, I'll do it."
"That's fine, fine, fine. . . ."

I kept my little girl's dolly voice alive for thirty years. "Yes,
sir, just leave it to me." "Wow, you look great, Fred." "Gee, I
hope the Vikings win for a change, Bob." Squeak, squeak,
squeal, squeal, smile, smile. I didn't give a damn about those
Vikings, but my whole life was like being a waitress in a
men's bar.

And the same with sex. "Yes, sure, anytime, Joe," "Fine, if
that makes you feel good, Fred," "Feel better now, Charlie?"

No wonder I became an addict: there was no me there to hold
on to, no center, no core, no voice of my own.

That's what I learned in the group. To make room for me and
create my own voice.

---

*I didn't think we were going to make it. All that baby
talk and that fake sweetness and acting out—it had
become a way of life. And it made us false together.
Now things are beginning to ring true.*

September 16
Idols

Let me look, just once more.

Why?

I adore those women, I want them to be mine.

> *You want them to be **like** you, you mean. Don't you see they're different?*

How, different? I identify with them, and I almost worship them.

> *You worship only what is like you. You bring everything back to yourself, to your own image.*

Well, that's my addiction, I guess.

> *Yes. You just dote on things that will bring **you** pleasure. Why not recognize the variety and difference in other people?*

That makes sense. I guess you're right. It's good to hear your friendly voice again.

> *Great! We'll make it, if we keep listening to each other.*

Yes. And thanks for helping me smash those idols.

I'm scared about my new job, you know. All those kids.

>*Of course. But you know you're a good teacher.*

I guess so. But every time I get a poor evaluation, I feel sick.
Then I want to run off and act out. Find myself a real man, a
real person.

>*A phantom.*

Yes.

>*Does that make you feel better, chasing ghosts?*

You know it doesn't. But anxiety sets me off, somehow. I
think if I get high on sex I'll feel better.

>*And do you feel better?*

Sometimes.

>*Sure?*

Well, no, not really. In fact, not much. Not at all. Never.

>*Never?*

Never.

>*Well, that was a good way out of that crisis. We used to
>fight and shout, and then you'd act out for sure.*

I know. Things can change. Talking changes things.

>*Yes. We're changing. And by the way, the kids loved
>that trip you took them on last week.*

September 18
Self-esteem

You know, I feel better every day. I swim, I walk, I meet with people in the group. I'm planning a retreat in the fall. What's happening?

Why don't you think you deserve these feelings?

Right on target! I'm not sure I'm worth all this happiness. It makes me scared. Reminds me of all those animals I loved and lost when I was a kid, and then Steve going off like that with my best friend. But I am happy, I feel it. Only . . .

Hold on. Do you realize what you just said?

Yes. I am happy. I feel it.

Hold on to that. Keep the feeling alive, hold it like a flower, nurture it like a garden, love it like a child. It's a precious gift, and one you deserve.

Thanks. I didn't expect such support from you!

Now, now! No more negative thoughts about our relationship. I'm sharing in this happiness, too, you know, and it's doing us both a world of good.

I used to collect women and stash them away in the storehouse of my mind like precious little art objects.

On rainy days I took them out and admired myself through my collection. Mine! All mine!

I was in love, of course, but it was a one-way street leading to my own safe little museum. And I went there just to love myself.

Art is art and people are people, that's what I've had to learn. Every now and again I'm still tempted to add another picture to my collection, but I soon wake up and realize what I'm doing.

Life is a celebration of humanness and difference, a celebration, not a collection.

> *I'd encourage your collecting habits, of course, with my Maternal voice: "Keep them safely locked up, and you'll be faithful only to Me." Well, you've broken the spell, and I'm glad for you. That dusty old museum was boring, you know.*

Boring for you, too?

> *Boring for both of us.*

September 20
Image, reality, and freedom

When I was addicted to pornography, I was glued to suggestive images and words as if they were the only reality.

I wanted to blot out everything in the real world and pretend that beyond pornography there was nothing. The sign **was** the object; the image **was** the truth. There was no other reality for me.

Absorbed by signs and images, I didn't want to reach out and relate to anyone real. I wanted the whole world to be just a shimmering reflection of my desire for pornography. I lived in a world of silence and shame.

Now the spell is broken. In my group and with my new friends, I am beginning to allow other people to have their own independence and their own freedom. No image can contain or capture them.

I see now that pictures, TV, advertisements, books, and films are only symbols, not reality. The real world is where I want to live, where people are individuals living in openness and freedom.

I remember how you used to be hypnotized by pornography and closed off from the world. I couldn't get through to you, partly because I was always beating on you. Now that things are changing, we can work on our relationship, too.

I remember as a kid falling in love with silky garments and wrapping them round my body to change my identity.

Swathed in silk, I was a new person, sexy, alluring, omnipotent.

Gradually I couldn't get excited without my swirling disguise. I was in love with the object of my own desires.

Then the disguise became a ritual that was enough to set me off in my adventures of acting out.

But I didn't want to share my precious objects with anyone else, and the same was true for my body. Mine, all mine!

Now, thanks to my recovery program, I can have a relationship with another person and not just a thing.

It feels good to be in love with the world and not with its objects.

> *Yes, those were strange days and strange gods. It feels good to be living with a real person at last!*

Thanks for saying that.

> *Thanks for being you.*

September 22
Distance

When I watch TV, I feel close to the characters, especially the women. I identify with them, and sometimes I even find myself speaking back to them as I watch the movie.

Then my husband comes home and I clam up. Oh, I chatter away all right, ask him about his day, tell him about the neighbors, you know, the little things.

The big things in my life are all on TV.

It was the same at home, in my family, ever since. . . ever since Dad was arrested for incest with Peggy, my older sister.

Incest! I hate the word. It hurts and cuts me. Imagine, Dad in bed with my sister, doing **that.**

My husband and I have separate rooms.

And I've got the TV.

You deserve the TV, darling. It's made for you. You'll never be comfortable with yourself and your body. Never. So just curl up and live your life on the little screen. It's just for you.

I used to love being thought of as a Casanova, always there, always ready, always available.

Women loved it, or so I thought. It was as if they were mesmerized by all the other women I'd had and all the great stories of my conquests.

And then one day on a trip, I met this woman on a plane who just sat there and laughed when I tried the same old routine. She didn't say anything, just laughed. The more I came on strong, the more she laughed.

I said: "What's the big idea?"

"You're the Big Idea. Nothing but an idea. Why can't you be a man, a human being?"

I tried to laugh it off, but it didn't work. And then, the funny thing is we started talking, not the same old stuff, but really serious and intimate. And we talked all night. Just talked.

I never saw her again, but I left my mask back there on that airplane. And it feels good to be me, just me.

Yes, I remember. You were a pain in those days, with your big mouth and your little fears. I'm glad you're back in the land of the sane. It's much more fun to live with a human being, not a Big Idea!

September 24
Lover boy

I t's taken me three years to say this simple statement: "When I was a boy, my mother wanted me to be her lover."

> *It sounds crazy, I agree. But now you can say it, and that's a start.*

Yes. I can say it to you, and I can say it out loud in my group. And they don't laugh, and neither do you.

> *Is that what you were scared of?*

That, and being disloyal.

> *Disloyal to whom?*

To Dad, of course.

> *You mean, you did. . . .*

No. I couldn't. You know that. You knew it then. You knew everything. But you gave me hell anyway, just for wanting to.

> *Yes. I remember, and I'm really sorry. But someone had to stick up for Dad.*

If Dad had been really **there,** he could have stood up for himself.

> *Isn't that a bit disloyal?*

No. It's the truth.

> *Good! Great! Fantastic! That's what we've both being dying to hear . . . and almost dying of guilt because we didn't hear it. Let's take this moment and run with it, run on till we're healed!*

Those of us who work in Twelve Step groups recognize that the final Step requires us to reach out and talk to others who are afflicted with our addiction.

We go and meet other people and tell them about our program and what it has meant to us.

I used to be afraid to make myself vulnerable in this way, for it means talking about my crazy sex addiction with a complete stranger. What if he called the cops? What if he laughed in my face?

I know now what the Program is all about: reaching out and sharing fears and hopes, shame and confidence. Building confidence.

In a way, we are always Twelve Stepping on our road to recovery.

> *Well, you didn't used to talk like that. You were always hiding away and letting me beat up on you. There's a new strength here, and I'm glad to share in it.*

September 26
Being patient

I get up and feel full of energy and desire for change. Yet I look in the mirror and see the same old face.

At breakfast I get into a fight. I don't apologize, I let things fester.

Later I want to act out. Maybe I do, just to get back at my parents. What's the use? What's the difference? It serves them right.

Wait a minute. That's not the way to get better. That sounds like my addicted self speaking. That's the same old story. And I'm tired of listening to that voice and that yarn.

I have time. If I take things easy, I can get in touch with what I really mean, what I really want. I can take time to change.

That's it. Gently does it. Let's not beat on you. Let's slow down, check things out, phone a friend, get that energy moving toward change. Nothing happens overnight. To change takes time, and you've got time. You said so yourself, and you'd better believe it!

I can't see myself clearly. I'm split and always on the move and full of strife.

> *Yes, I know it's hard. It seems like a losing battle.*

Hey, wait a minute. Don't you let me down, too, just when I need you. I thought you were on my side now.

> *Okay, let's talk. What do you want to see, to understand, to know?*

Why I act out. And who is this "I" anyway—a voice, a feeling, a person, a world?

> *All of the above and none of the above. You're lots of voices, but one person, and yet always changing.*

That's it. So how can "I" know this other person who's always changing?

> *You don't just know—you feel, think, talk, move, invent, create. You're not a thing, you're an adventure!*

So?

> *So . . . be it.*

Explain!

> *Why do you want to explain everything? I'm trying to say that you and I and all our voices and scripts make up our being. And the adventure of life is being . . . an adventure. And we're still writing it!*

September 28
Obsession

I used to spend half my life lost in fantasies about sex. Work, friends, children, affection, play—all were sacrificed to fantasies and acting out.

I sometimes spent a whole afternoon away from work, cruising or rummaging around in pornographic bookshops. The less satisfied I was, the more I dwelled on sex.

I was like a sleepwalker, only half alive.

In recovery I woke up. I met people who had lived the same kind of lonely, addictive lives, and I saw how they had found new ways of coping with sadness and loneliness.

Joining a group was the best thing I've ever done. I'm alive now and free to make my own choices about how I want to live.

> *It's true, you were like a zombie. But don't forget, I made things worse, never missing a chance to make you feel bad.*

Why did you do that?

> *I was obsessed, too—obsessed with power and control.*

And now?

> *I'm waking up too—waking up to life!*

I look at myself and think, "God, why don't I ever measure up to what Dad wanted?" Or, "I know Mom would be disappointed in me if she really knew what I was like." They were always on me to do better, to be better. Criticizing and carping.

How deep these wounds have gone, and how carefully I've tried to patch them over with my brilliant perfectionist constructions.

And then, of course, I fall short, and I punish myself—perhaps I even take pleasure in punishing myself because that's what I'm used to.

But it doesn't have to be like that.

I am learning what it means to be human—to be weak as well as strong, idle as well as efficient, hesitant as well as confident. If I have a slip, it's not the end of the world; it's time for forgiveness and love.

It's always time for forgiveness and love.

> *You sound a bit smug, still. You still have a long way to go before you really deserve forgiveness.*

What a boring old man you are sometimes!

September 30
Friends

*H*ow are you today, young man?

I'm fine, thanks, old boy.

> *Who are you calling old?*

Well, for as long as I can remember, you've been the old watchdog, the old guard.

> *I suppose that's true. And what a tyrant I used to be!*

You said it.

> *And you?*

And what a spoiled and self-indulgent brat I used to be!

> *I'm glad we agree on our past.*

And I'm glad we agree in the present.

> *Yes. What a difference it makes to be in recovery.*

Thanks to the Program.

> *And thanks to ourselves.*

Yes. That's true. We've both worked hard to get rid of those old voices, and create new ways of speaking to ourselves and to each other. I'm happy with that.

> *I'm happy with you.*

Me too!

274

I sought all the answers in sex, but I wasn't asking the right questions. I thought I'd find my identity in acting out, but I found only a role and a mask.

I used to read pornographic books and identify with the characters, and then I'd act out. I mistook the image for the reality—and the more I was disappointed, the more I persisted in the search.

I had things the wrong way 'round. I'm learning to create my individuality in loving relationships, in my group and with my friends.

Sex will always be a bit of a puzzle. But now I see it as an expression and an extension of my own identity and not its definition.

> *Yes, indeed! The more you acted out, the more you lost yourself. And you thought you were finding the truth.*

True. But don't forget that you didn't help much, either. How I loathed your bullying voice!

> *I know. I did give you a hard time. But now we're changing and solving the puzzle of our addiction.*

October 2
Blow-up

I think I'm going to need to look at my porno videos today.

> *How come?*

I like the power to freeze the images and make them mine.

> *They're just pictures, you know. They may seem larger than life, but in fact they demean life.*

Mind your own business. I'm a free agent.

> *How can you be addicted to pornography and a free agent?*

I'd kill you if I could—always on my back, jeering and sneering!

> *Look, we're in this together, and we can learn from each other.*

How can we learn when you're always criticizing?

> *No, listen, can't you hear the difference? I understand you better now, and I want both of us to make a breakthrough. Remember the Program and the Steps and the new power of the group. . . .*

Yes . . . I see . . . I was forgetting. Let's go on talking. This is all so new to me.

> *Great! We've been at war too long. It's a good feeling to begin a real dialogue.*

276

I used to be scared to find myself alone; I felt forsaken and desolate, isolated, and drifting toward death.

In relationships, I would do almost anything to hang on so that I wouldn't be on my own again. But I'd be abandoned anyway, like a child.

Many people in my group have said the same thing, and that helped me feel less alone. I realize I need to learn to get onto good terms with myself so that I can love from strength, not weakness.

Now I can see the difference between solitude and loneliness. In solitude I can truly be myself and like myself and not feel abandoned or scared.

These days, I like being alone, listening to my needs, even talking to myself.

Yes, and you're fun to talk to—a bit difficult sometimes, but then I guess we all are! Especially me! You are different now, less anxious, less scared; it's great to hang around with you. You know what? We're going to make it.

October 4
Limits

As a child I never knew where my world ended and other people began.

My mother nurtured, and tended . . . and trespassed and invaded and stifled me.

I did the same to my brother, because I loved playing little mother to my baby. "Cuddles," I called him.

When Cuddles grew up, he joined the army and then went into the ministry. He was arrested last week for abusing boys in the vestry.

I don't want to talk about this, because in a way it's none of my business.

I mean, the only way you can stay sane in this life is keeping your distance. I learned that the hard way.

But I miss him, my baby!

You're right. It isn't your business. You did the best you could, just like Mother. And one thing you know you can count on—Mother loves you, and she'll always be here for you.

In my addiction I loved to take risks, and I even sought danger. I felt smug. I liked to brag.

A couple of times I got really hurt, and then I knew I was out of control.

I remember thinking, "I can't go on like this, my life is hopeless, a mess."

I'm glad it wasn't too late. I'm really glad I made it.

Now the risks I take have to do with my recovery—honesty, vulnerability, reaching out, loving.

These are the risks worth taking.

> *Sure. Let's remember the bad old days and make sure they don't come back. Far too scary for me! I like it better now that we're on the road to sanity.*

It's good to be traveling together.

October 6
Spiritual

I used to think that being spiritual meant believing in the soul and the afterlife, forever and ever.

And now?

Now, I think that it's possible that, well, I mean . . . I might, you know, believe in, well, being spiritual.

Other worlds? Worlds of the spirit? Ghosts in the attic?

Don't tease me. No. This world. Being good. Striving to be good. Loving.

You sound embarrassed.

Yes, well, that's not my usual way of speaking, you know.

That's the Program speaking, you mean?

Yes, in a way. But I'm beginning to collaborate.

Yes, I hear you.

And it feels just fine, you know.

Yes, I do know. And it sounds good and feels good, for both of us.

I agree. For both of us.

Sex used to give me the same feelings of comfort, escape, excitement, and release that other people get from alcohol or drugs. It affected me physically as well as in my mind.

But after the high came the disgust and the shame. I knew I was being false to myself and not facing the real challenges of life. Sex as I distorted it was just an escape from growing up; it kept me infantile and dependent.

I wanted to be free—not free from sex but from its tyranny. I had to transform my feelings about myself and learn to relate to others in an adult way.

Then sex could become part of my life again, integrated into my relationships with myself, with others, and with the world.

> *You've learned a lot, haven't you, from working in your group. At first I sneered at you and called you a wimp for not doing it all by yourself. But you kept faith with the group, and I've come to respect you and even love you a bit!*

Well, that's nice to hear, especially from you, dear Supervoice.

October 8
Body

I like the bit in the marriage service where it says, "With my body I thee worship." The only trouble is that I don't think my body deserves it.

> *Doesn't deserve what?*

Worship. Love. Passion. I look at those ads, and I know there'll be no worship until I get my hair redone, breasts reduced, lines smoothed, thighs vacuumed, legs shaved, feet exchanged, a whole new self.

> *Sounds like a piece of real estate, your body!*

Well, that's what it feels like when I look at those ads. "Needs refurbishing, from top to toe." No wonder I act out with any man who even looks at me twice.

> *Yes, I know those image-makers put us down all the time. But don't forget, most of them are men who are probably terrified of a real woman. They prefer furniture.*

That's great! You're right. I'll try being myself for a change.

> *That's good enough for me. I like you as you are, and so do lots of other people, don't forget. Can we dare to let ourselves be loved for who we are?*

For a long time I knew I needed help. I went into therapy, and worked on my guilt and shame and my low self-esteem.

But I always kept my little secret, my private world of sexual fantasies and acting. It made me feel so powerful that not even my therapist could find me out.

At the same time, I felt ashamed—ashamed of my sex addiction and ashamed of myself. I used to pick up guys in the park and have sex with them in my car. For fun, not money, you understand.

And, to tell the truth, it wasn't much fun.

I didn't understand it and I couldn't talk about it. Till one day I began to get involved with one of my studs, as I used to call them. And then, out of the blue, he said: "I'm in this group for sex addicts. I think it might help you, too."

I didn't laugh. I listened. And went. And recovered. And married the guy.

Now we laugh about it sometimes. He says: "I said it first, you know." And I say: "Yes. Thanks. I know. But I was ready."

Yes, you were ready. And so was your Higher Power.

October 10
Minefield

Freud says . . .

> *Oh, Lord. Not him again!*

I hardly ever mention him.

> *True. You're getting healthy. Well, all right, what does Freud say?*

Freud says that unless a man can come to terms with the idea of committing incest with his mother or sister, he'll probably not be able to have a good, open, mature sexual relationship.

> *He's totally crazy. That fraud! If I've told you once, I've told you that a thousand times. But you will persist. You were always disobedient, dishonest, sly, lustful, voracious, degenerate, foul . . . You pervert, coward, beast . . .*

Hey! What happened? Your voice is metal, fire, shrapnel, knife-edge, sword. Let me be. Leave me be! It's always the same old story. Whenever I mention desire and Mother, you go off like a madman. Just listen. For me, Freud's right. Not because it's Freud, but because **I know what happened in my own life.** And I have to come to terms with that. I have to face it, and I'm going to face it. Alone if necessary. But I'd rather face it together with you.

> *Just let me get my breath back. There's something there that sets me off, drives me crazy. What? Yes, I think you're right: the truth.*

Talking things over

I used to find it difficult to talk to my friends or people in my group about my addiction.

Shame covered me with its ugly mask. I could never be natural and open and honest.

I learned to talk fearlessly for the first time in therapy, and then in my group. At first it was hard and painful. I felt shackled to my shame.

But practice helps. Gradually the words came and I could let go of the dark secrets of my acting out.

I began to feel light and free. I no longer carried the burdens of the past like sacks of concrete on my back.

I feel like dancing and leaping for joy!

> *Yes. It's great to let go and feel happy and free.*

And you, old man, can you dance?

> *I'm learning!*

October 12
Apathy

I don't feel like doing much today.

> *You never do, you know. You were born lazy.*

I feel so tired and I've done nothing.

> *That's you all over—good for nothing. Why not look at some of your dad's pornography?*

Why not? That'll get me going.

> *See? Excited now, eh?*

No. It makes me feel lethargic and hopeless. It's not pleasure, it's addiction. That's it, I'm an addict. I can't go on like this, I'm going to do something about it. My life's unmanageable.

> *Yes, you're right. It always will be. Your life's a dead end.*

Not anymore. I've hit bottom, and now I'm going to take the First Step and really get my life moving again. You'll see.

> *I'll be watching.*

Waiting for me to fail?

> *We'll see.*

What a strange expression—"acting out." Where does it come from? What does it mean?

In our obsessions we build up scenarios, like scenes in a play or a movie, with their own gestures and scripts and actions.

Mine are always the same . . . and I'm always in the center, the focus of attention.

The pressure gets to me, my blood starts beating, I have to find release, I can't contain this tension anymore. I must act, act out.

I see the power of this, and it made my life totally unmanageable.

I'm ready to take the First Step to save my sanity, even perhaps my life.

I'm not sure we're going to make it. You've come to love being a playboy and an actor. How do you know who you are anymore?

October 14
Relaxing

I should do this, I ought to that, I nearly forgot, I must get going, I'll never finish . . . rush, rush, rush . . . and then we die. The end.

What a story! How dramatic! How absurd!

What about the world? My friends? My loved ones? Myself? Haven't I got time for them?

What do I do with all the time I saved rushing about? Rush about some more?

Enough! I'm not going to go on like this. I need to take time to look and listen and talk and laze and drift and dream and talk some more and read and think and take things easy.

Part of my recovery is letting go, slowing down, living in the present, opening my eyes to the beauty of the world.

How good it feels to enjoy and savor life again!

Yes, you were pretty crazy, back then! But now you're changing, and it's good for me to be around you and watch you slowing down and beginning to let go. I'm learning to relax as well, you know.

You know, you're really funny.

> *Funny peculiar or funny ha-ha?*

Weird . . . and you make me laugh.

> *At anything in particular?*

Yes, your voice. It sounds so clipped, so precise, so British.

> *That's my Victorian voice, don't you know. The one that kept the Empire in order and the flag flying.*

While the prostitutes invaded the London streets.

> *Yes, Empire and addicts . . . they do seem to go together.*

Just like us in the old days.

> *Yes. I tried to play the policeman on sex, and you tried to give me the slip.*

And then the slips became habits. And the habits a way of life. And then . . . the prostitutes, night after night.

> *And now?*

The Empire is over, and so is the addiction!

> *The Empire is over. Long live the Empire!*

Long live love!

October 16
Needs

I never thought anyone cared about my needs or even that they could be met. As a child, I was afraid to say what I needed because I always felt ignored or criticized.

So I hid my needs from others and sought to satisfy them in lonely sex. And my needs only became greater. More sex, more fear, more need.

I didn't trust other people, so I allowed myself to be sexually humiliated.

I thought this pain would go on forever. "That's life," I would say.

Now, in recovery, I'm not afraid to say that I have real needs like anyone else. I am learning to express them and ask for them to be met.

And there are people who listen and respond.

> *I felt your pain, but I couldn't help. I was too busy playing the heavy parent.*

And I was the wayward child.

> *What a crazy pair we were!*

But now our voices are changing.

At home everyone was addicted—to food, tobacco, buying things, pornography, booze, sex, drugs. It was like a mad carnival, a frenzy from morning till night.

That's not an excuse, it's a fact. I don't know why or how, but we all had to have our highs. "Choose your addiction," that was the unspoken motto of the family.

I chose sex. Books, pictures, underwear, porno booths, johns, parks, wherever there was sex, I went. And the more the risk the greater the thrill. I craved the danger and the high and the anonymity of the encounters.

I lost my job, beat up my wife, abandoned my kids, almost went crazy—a nightmare, not a life.

I don't want to die like this, to end my life with this rage and fear.

Where can I find help?

> *Let's talk about this, now, tomorrow, every day. I've been encouraging you in your craziness, and now we're both bankrupt. There are programs, groups, support—let's go for help. It could be the only way.*

Yes. There must be a way, a path, a new journey.

October 18
Silence

When I left home I thought I was in pretty good shape. We never had fights, we never got emotional, we never talked about anything uncomfortable.

I went to college and dated this guy. One day he came on strong and I kind of went along for a while. You know, heavy petting and all that. Then he started taking off my blouse, and I told him to stop. His face went red and he called me a prick-tease. And then he told me I had led him on; I had to go the whole way. He scared me, and I did what he wanted.

I told a girl friend, and she said I had been raped. I was angry, but I didn't know what to do about it. I felt it was kind of my fault. I did nothing.

Since then, the only sex I've had is with myself. And I'm even scared about that now.

> *Your girl friend is right. We've been silent too long, you and I. We need to talk.*

Yes. And we need help.

You don't sound so loud today.

> *I don't feel so loud.*

Then that's good for both of us.

> *Yes. It's because of Dad.*

Dad's dying, you mean?

> *Dad's dying and my remembering. It's been five years, but I still think about it. How brave he was right up to the end.*

Yes. I loved him, finally.

> *It's been hard, hasn't it, especially since I kept his angry voice alive for so long.*

Yes. I hated and feared that voice of his, that voice of yours. It's been hard. Very hard. But hard for both of us. It must have been lonely and sad for you to have to play the part of judge and executioner.

> *I'm glad you understand that.*

And now we're talking in a rational, friendly, understanding way. It's going to get better and better, you'll see.

> *Yes. We're making some new tapes together.*

October 20
Debate

I want to go off and look at some magazines.

> *Wait a minute. That's one of the boundaries you set up in the group, isn't it?*

Well, not exactly. I said I wasn't going to read anymore of those hard-core books. It's not really the same. I mean these are just pictures of women . . . you know, arty kinds of pictures.

> *Sure. I know the kind of pictures. Your Dad's study was full of them. But why do you need them? And why now?*

I'm writing this paper for English class. And I'm stuck.

> *So you need inspiration!*

It's not that. It relaxes me.

> *And then you masturbate.*

Well, not every time.

> *Nine times out of ten. I've counted.*

You know, you're not a friend. You're a policeman. If you can't trust me, how do expect me to get better and get on with my life? I'm a grown-up man, you know. It's just that we all need a little pleasure.

> *You argue like a child, but I'm trying not to keep on treating you like a child. If we want to heal ourselves from this sex addiction, we're going to need to carry on some rational conversations. I want to try. How about you?*

I'll give it some thought.

I've loved him totally ever since I saw him on the "Teen Queen" show last November 29th, at 6:45 in the evening, to be precise. I was baby-sitting Sherri and he came on the screen with his Frenzied Jello group, and he turned me into instant marshmallow whip.

Talk about Cinderella in reverse. I was doing fine at school and I had this friend Mike as a steady date. I was working at Star Kingfisheries five days a week in the evenings to pay for my car, and I was in the choir at Sunday School. Everything went to dust and ashes over night.

I need help. It's crazy. There's no space inside me, no room for me, or for Dad or Mom, or friends, or pets, or fresh air, or anything. I dream of him, need him, breathe him.

I don't want to touch anyone real.

I need help. But I need him more.

You're right. It's like a spell, this fantasy. You're losing your grip on life. We need to talk this over with other women and get help.

October 22
Recall

Sex addicts talk about "euphoric recall"—the thrill of replaying in fantasy a sexual encounter. Now, in the mind, everything is excitement and delight and luxury and pleasure.

In such fantasies, real human elements (affection, timidity, touch, support, tenderness) are juggled away; all that remains is **my** pleasure, **my** success, **my** safety. The other person disappears in the smoke screen of my euphoric fantasy.

I am learning to remember the past in a different way, in all its human complexity and fullness. I don't want to see the past only as it affects me and my fictitious pleasures.

Life is too rich and complex to reduce everything to a single, fake emotion. Joy and sadness, love and loss, and not just euphoria, are the reality of a person's life.

Yes, I remember, you thought only of yourself and the next fix. And it always let you down, down into the pit of self-loathing and disgust. And then you were at my mercy. Now we can go forward together, affectionately, secure in our understanding of the past.

I hated the end of school, all those tests and report cards.

That's the first thing Dad wanted to see. Scowl, scowl.

"Got to do better, kid. Look at your brother."

I was sick and tired of looking at him.

"Go to your room! You're grounded."

I needed help, not punishment. Help!

"Stay in your room." Grounded.

Anger, comparisons, criticism, scowls.

I found a place just for me, my own secret world of sex. Risks and thrills, and a world in my own image, not my brother's. Oh, the power and the pleasure of it! My world. All mine!

The world of the addict.

> *Simple, really. And I was always there, taking over
> Dad's voice, keeping you scared and shameful.*

Yes. Scared and shameful.

> *And now?*

Let's talk.

> *And work.*

And play. Let's not forget to play.

> *And recover our childhood.*

October 24
Abstraction

Sometimes it's good to withdraw from the hurly-burly of the world and seek safety and power in detached thinking. Often it's a way of coping with anxiety—a necessary defense.

Thinking is not the same as fantasy where I lose myself in images of self-gratification and often act out.

I need to establish some distance from the world, at times, and I can find satisfaction, as the scientist does, in the deep pleasure of abstract thinking.

Then, I can move out into the world again, strengthened, to participate in life around me.

I used to laugh at you for running away and hiding behind abstractions. Now I can see that we need times of contemplation as well as times of action.

Part of my addiction was the need to betray the person I was living with. It's hard to think of that even now, but I couldn't be content until I'd let my lover down.

I'd come home after acting out and get a cruel pleasure in inventing a lie. I looked my lover in the eye and betrayed the trust I saw there.

Addiction does that. It makes you look at someone you love and deny the truth and intimacy between you.

There's only one way out. Win back the trust. Learn to trust myself and my group, my program, my friends in recovery. Trust brings love and love defeats addiction.

It's easy to say and hard to do. But it can be done by following the Twelve Step path. It takes time and patience and courage to win back that trust, but it's worth it.

Now I can look someone in the eye and feel the love clear and strong, beyond betrayal.

Agreed. But who am I going to shout at now?

Nobody.

I can live with that.

I sure can, too!

October 26
Help

You seem rather quiet these days.

> *I'm not feeling so good, if you want to know.*

I do want to know. Really.

> *I feel isolated. In the cold. Lonely.*

Why? What's happened?

> *Ever since you've been in that group of yours, you've been strong, independent, outgoing. . . .*

I know. I've been feeling really powerful. Where does that leave you?

> *Exactly. That's what I'm trying to figure out. I always thought you were dependent on me, but I think it may have been the other way around.*

Don't tell me you're a raving codependent, you, Mr. Supervoice! Well, speak up, man, don't just stand there sniveling!

> *Mock not, lest ye be mocked! And remember that's my specialty.*

Not anymore. We don't have to have a specialty—mockery. Let's just concentrate on one thing—being human. I'm sure that'll give us plenty to talk about.

> *Agreed! And thanks for jolting me out of my gloom. It will be great having an adult around to talk to, instead of an addicted little child.*

In my sex addiction I was always out of control, never knowing from one hour to the next whether I was going to act out.

Sometimes when I was driving home, feeling good, I suddenly found myself in a place that brought me only guilt and shame.

When I was out of control like that, I couldn't rely on myself and I didn't trust myself. I felt lost and divided inside.

It's been hard to learn to trust myself after all that furtive peeping and anonymous encounters. But now, as I recover, I'm learning to like myself and gain confidence in my Higher Power.

I speak to myself gently and kindly each day. It feels good to know I am more in touch with myself and healing the split within me.

It's trust that heals us.

Trust and love.

October 28
Pressures

As a child I always felt pressure to be good, to be obedient, to succeed, to please. And then, there were hidden pressures and tensions in the family that increased my anxiety whenever I fell short of perfection.

Sex became a drug, an anesthetic. I would masturbate to escape and try to get rid of the pressures, but of course they only came back more strongly, because of my guilt.

Pressure, sex, guilt, pressure, sex, guilt—that was the pattern and the ritual. And I felt I would never escape.

I could never have broken free without the group.

I need the strength that comes from tolerance and disinterested love. I feel powerful in a program where there are no anxious pressures, only the step-by-step affirmative movement toward sanity and new power.

> *How I loved those pressures—they kept you in my power. I was the angry parent and you were the wayward child. I knew everything about you and made you pay for all your sins.*

And you loved doing that, didn't you! But now you're changing, too.

For sex addicts, abstinence is often a necessary part of the journey toward recovery.

This scares some people—"What! No sex! Thanks a lot, not for me!"

But we're talking about the change from uncontrollable sexual behavior to a sexuality that is ours to withhold or share. And often a period of abstinence is a necessary step and a time to take stock.

Then we can move forward and outward into the world, knowing that our sexuality belongs to us rather than owning us.

I feel fine with that and it's helped me through.

> *Well, that's a change! You used to ramble on about free love and sexual experimentation as if the whole world were just one huge sexual bazaar!*

How infantile I was!

> *Yes. You thought you knew it all.*

And you?

> *I knew I knew it all!*

The blind leading the blind!

October 30
Critical thinking

*E*veryone in the group likes you, you know.

Except you.

> *Wait a minute! Just because I used to be your harshest critic.*

You were more than a critic, you know. You were a sadist. And the more I wanted to act out, the more you raged at me.

> *Yes I know. I couldn't help it. There was some mysterious link between your lust and my anger. It started when you were a kid in love with Mom.*

Don't be ridiculous! I wasn't in love with Mom.

> *And I took over the role of Dad.*

Really! All this stupid pop psychology. I just want us to be friends, you and I.

> *Well, we have to understand each other first.*

Do you really think I was in love with Mom?

> *What do you think?*

It doesn't seem possible. I was too young. Well, of course I loved her. I'll have to think about it. There's nothing wrong in it. Maybe you're right.

> *I thought this conversation would freak you out. It must be that "tough love" they talk about in our group.*

I used to be able to get my way by turning on the charm. People responded, and then I entangled them in my own sexual scenarios.

I guess many sex addicts operate that way. And the Casanovas and Don Juans among us usually end up by getting what we desire.

That kind of success doesn't last, though—and that's perhaps secretly what we want. We want to be able to move on when our partners make adult demands on us. Other people expect us to treat them with respect, affection, and caring; and all we care about is pleasure and sex.

A program of recovery teaches us commitment, trust, affection, and loyalty. We keep coming back and are made to feel wanted for who we are. And others come back to see us and greet us.

That's the difference between caring and charming. Caring, like the Program, endures.

> *Well, that's new! You didn't speak like that in the good old days. This is a new voice I'm hearing. What's happening?*

The charm is wearing off!

November 1
Free association

When I was in my addiction, I'd come home after a hard day at the office, mix myself a stiff drink, turn on some really sexy country music, and just hang loose and let my thoughts wander.

I knew I'd always end up in the same mental place—the place where I liked to go and be looked at.

I'd never go there directly. Part of the fun was just letting my thoughts circle around, like a hawk around its prey, knowing that in the end I'd be there, in that special place.

And then, after a couple of drinks, I'd call a cab and go there.

And pick up a guy, go home with him, and have some fun.

I told that story several times in the group. Each time I said the word "fun," I cried. And each time I felt the energy and love of the group encircle me.

That's my free association now. The group.

---

*That's the place I like to be with you the most these days. And that's where **our** association is getting stronger every time.*

As a sex addict I used to lead a life of desperation, taking risks with my body, my spirit, and with people I cared for.

I hid myself away from the open glance of affection and the dynamic interaction of love.

All I cared about was my own pleasure; and in my search for continual highs, I hurt other people and did myself harm.

This was my secret and my shame. I loved and hated my secret life.

Now I have to come to see that secrets give force and encouragement to my addiction. They are the driving power of my shame.

Talking things over with others banishes the power of the secret and opens me out to the world.

In openness and honesty I can walk without shame and find love and peace.

You thought you were safe in your secret life, but really you were in great danger. I was scared for you and that made me anxious and brutal. I'm glad we're in recovery.

November 3
Party line

I feel lonely and down. I need that high again.

Do you feel mad, sad, or bad?

Mad, mostly.

Can't you focus your anger?

No. I'm just mad. Mad at myself. Mad at the world.

Anger can be productive, you know.

How?

It can help make things clear. But you've got to focus.

You keep saying that. But what does it mean?

Now, now. You sound angry.

But I thought anger was productive.

Yes. But not if you're angry at me. You can't focus on me; I'm part of you. Anyway, I'm not the cause of your problems.

Not all of them, I agree. But let me tell you one thing. You sound like the prosecutor, judge, and jury. You always know everything, standing there on your pedestal. Why can't you be human, too, instead of just spouting the party line?

*Well, well. And I thought we were on the same side. You've a lot to learn, you know. And you **can** learn, if only you'd listen. And then focus, focus that anger of yours.*

When I was a child, we were always moving around. My dad was in the army, and every two years or so, we would pull up stakes and move on.

I had to leave my school, the community in which I was just getting settled, my pets, my friends.

I coped by acting out, trying to medicate the feelings of separation and loss. And then, later, whenever I was going to leave or be left, I acted out in the same way. Compulsive repetition.

Now I have found in my group a stable community and friends who are there for me, day after day, week after week.

I don't feel lost or abandoned, so there's no need to act out anymore.

I'm putting down roots.

> *Yes, I remember those bad old days. And I dumped on you, just like Dad, and make you feel bad for being such a baby.*

Well, I behaved like a baby.

> *Not anymore.*

November 5
Perspective

After my divorce, I felt as though all the springs of my life had dried up. We didn't have any kids together, and there was no need for me to keep in touch with my ex-husband. So I didn't.

In fact, I broke off with all our friends. I wanted to make a fresh start. I'd been far too dependent on Joe and the gang.

So I was going to go it alone. I needed to be alone and find myself as a woman and get some perspective on my life.

And then I met this guy at the health club. In the sauna, of all places. I lusted for his body before I could see his face through the steam.

Fred was available all right. We had sex the second time we met, and then we backed off a little and tried to get to know each other. But the sex kept getting in the way. We never seemed to have time to talk and laze and be just plain affectionate.

We broke up. And since then, I've had four affairs and the pattern is always the same. Sex. Sex. Sex.

And beyond that, nothing. Except shame.

We really do need to spend some time alone, you and I. We need a time of abstinence, a time for us.

You know, it's no big deal to fall in love. It's just a game and it never lasts.

> *That's it. We need to keep on moving along. Otherwise we'll get stale.*

Right. And people really aren't all that interesting once you get to know them. The glamor soon wears off.

> *Sure. And it's really more fun to be alone, just the two of us.*

Yeah. At least there's no risk and no letdown.

> *And it means you'll always be faithful to the person who really counts, your mom.*

Wait. That's crazy, I'm thirty now. It's time I learned to stand on my own feet. I'm going to do something in my program to change all that. It's time I moved on to find out who I really am and what I need.

Not for Mom, but for me.

> *She'll still be there, you know.*

I know. But as an adult, not a parent.

> *Once a parent, always a parent.*

Speak for yourself, Supermom!

November 7
Humiliation and humility

As a child I felt humiliated by sexual messages that came to me unbidden and unwanted.

Adults around me responded to my playfulness and tenderness with inappropriate words, gestures, and actions. I felt wounded in the quick of my sexuality.

For years I masked my pain with grandiose words and aggressive behavior. I thought I could fight my way free of humiliation.

Gradually I came to realize that I was powerless to control the addiction that was devastating my life. I needed help and a new source of power.

I turned toward others and found strength and support in a Twelve Step Program. I learned that as an addict my life was hopeless and unmanageable. My new friends helped me see the difference between humiliation and humility.

> *You were sexually abused as a child. And I helped keep the humiliation and pain alive.*

Why? Why?

> *I was programmed, too, you know.*

Let's work the **new** Program together, shall we?

> *Yes.*

312

You know, you're still on the same old path.
And you're still talking in the same old voice.

> *How do you mean?*

Sneering and jeering.

> *Well, I suppose that's force of habit.*

You can change, too, you know.

> *Yes, you're right. I've been too busy spying on you to notice my own tone of voice. What do you suggest?*

How about more patience and tolerance.

> *Oh, I see, you just want me to let you off the hook.*

There you go again. Why not try to be on **our** side for a change?

> **Our** *side? What's* **our** *side?*

The side of tolerance and helpfulness.

> *I like that idea. A new direction.*

New direction, new voices.

November 9
Strangers

How often I used to seek out strangers to act out with. I knew it was a risk, but that was part of the thrill.

I didn't want to know them or have any follow-up. I just wanted to feed my addiction and make myself feel good.

The only snag was . . . afterwards. I always felt down, and then I heard those scornful, damning voices inside me. "You're lonely, scared, hopeless, worthless, bankrupt." I felt like a stranger to myself, an outsider.

I don't need those voices and now I hardly ever hear them. Not because they simply went away, but because I changed my behavior.

I've learned to take care of myself, to feel pride, affection, self-worth. I've been working the Program and talking to others in the group who used to feel as I did.

These people are not strangers, even though outside the group I hardly know them. They are new friends and new voices who have helped me banish the stranger within.

> *We were strangers to each other, too.*

And now?

> *Brothers.*

I'd just like to stop. I just really want to stop. It's just . . .

> *There's that word again!*

Which word again, my dear Supervoice?

> *The "just" word—that hasn't anything to do with justice.*

Well, it's just that I. . . .

> *There you go again.*

What's wrong with it?

> *It's just that you use it as an excuse.*

Now **you're** doing it. An excuse for what?

> *For wanting something without being willing to really go for it.*

Like what?

> *Recovery. Health. Sanity. Love.*

Yes. I see what you mean. And you're right. It's just. . . .

> *Justice, you mean!*

November 11
Adventure

A true sexual relationship always contains an element of the unknown. We meet at a level that is full of adventure, even risk.

I used to think that acting out was real because of the risk. And often someone got hurt, and then there was anger and hostility and hasty departures.

Addiction brings thrills and adventures of a kind—but they never endure and rarely leave good feelings behind. That's because we are never really there for our partners or even ourselves.

Now I realize that the risks of sex addiction are risks not worth taking. So many of us end up lonely and hurt and full of shame.

I'm glad I've moved from the sick thrill of addiction to the risks and adventures of a real relationship.

> *Am I included?*

Do you want to risk it?

> *Yes!*

You know he's not suitable, don't you?

I love him.

> *Don't be silly, dear. You hardly know him. You just threw yourself at him.*

I've known him for a year. And I love him.

> *He's weak. And then he's too old for you.*

He's only four years older than me. Dad was ten years older than you!

> *That was part of the trouble. He treated me like a child.*

And now you're treating me like a child!

> *Don't behave like one, then.*

You're making me very angry.

> *That proves I'm right.*

No. You're not right. I'm angry because you're still interfering in my life. And I'm a grown woman. And you're dead.

> *It makes no difference. I still love you, and I'm still inside you, part of you. I won't leave you, darling. Ever.*

November 13
Recovering

When I was in my sex addiction, I often felt covered in shame as a result of my selfish and hurtful actions.

Now I am working in a Program to get well again; I feel as if I am on a voyage of discovery. Secrets I had hidden for years are out in the open, and I am learning to deal honestly with my past.

Being able to talk openly and fearlessly about myself means that shame is withering away in the clear light of day. I am shedding old skins like a snake renewing itself.

Recovery is learning to create new feelings and ideas about myself and the world.

> *Yes, we both see changes happening. Shame kept us hidden and apart.*

Blind.

> *Dumb.*

Dumb.

> *Blind.*

I'm glad we agree, at last!

Here's a scenario I can't get away from.

Tell me.

Here's a mother humiliated in her sexuality. Seeks revenge, unconsciously, by humiliating her son.

How?

She seduces him in a thousand ways—oh, nothing overt . . . glances, gestures, scarlet panties, a little perverting striptease here and there.

You're joking!

Oh, no. It's simple. The half-closed door, the muffled call, the endless promptings of desire for his desire. . . .

And then?

The door slams on his penis!

Ouch!

Not literally, of course; figuratively. The mother's sex weaves desire, impossibility, and punishment together in a single figure—and presides over it.

Castration!

Ouch! **Must** you use these technical terms!

This really scares the hell out of both of us. We need to act this out, not in our addiction, but in words. Then we can begin to figure it out together.

November 15
The beauty of the world

When I was lost in my sex addiction, I was so self-absorbed that the world around me became a vague and shadowy place.

The images that crowded into my mind were fantasy images always available for control and exploitation.

I didn't look outward at the world; I never walked contentedly in nature. My gaze was always inward and self-concerned.

Now, in recovery, I am learning to look at people as people and not as objects of exploitation. I see things, I notice things, I am getting a sense of how things look and how they are.

In nature, now, I watch and listen and take in the beauty of a cloud soaring, a bird in flight, a new shoot on a lilac bush, a golden bank of flowers.

I feel in touch with the world again.

You are different now. This change is affecting me, too. I don't feel so aloof and hostile. I'm even learning to speak kindly to you, now and again!

*Y*ou've missed the group twice this month, you know.

What of it?

> *Well, didn't you make a commitment to go there for six weeks and see how you liked it?*

Mind your own business.

> *I thought we decided to make it our business.*

I don't remember that, and anyway I'm old enough to decide these things for myself without your playing the "Daddy" role.

> *I think you're trying to avoid the issue.*

That's the way you see it. You never see things from my point of view.

> *What's your point of view on this particular issue, then?*

I don't like being bullied.

> *That's not really the issue, is it? Let's be fair. We're talking about going to the group.*

You are, you mean. And that's your problem.

> *Let's agree to drop the matter for now. But we owe it to each other to talk this out. Let's think about it and try to talk again tomorrow after breakfast, shall we?*

November 17
Medication

Addicts speak about the need to take care of their grief or pain. That is a real need for everyone, but we used our addiction to medicate our feelings of hurt.

We ran from pain toward an imagined world of endless pleasure.

My addiction became my prescription, my medicine, my attendant, and finally my jailer. After a while I needed medication for my addiction, and I couldn't find any. I hit bottom where there was no relief, no more medication.

The way out was to change systems and change medicines: the group, not the ego; love, not addiction.

I must say, I couldn't help laughing as you dashed around like a madman, seeking one fix after another! What a fool you were, and what a sadist I was, enjoying feeling your pain. Now thank God, all that's in the past.

It's her hair, you know, I could spin it into shining raiment.

And then, her feet, they're so slim and delicate, like a child's really. I want to hold them and bathe them, be her mother or sister.

She's beautiful and cruel, too. I'd like to be her child.

And get punished.

She's so much finer than I am, gifted, really brilliant, shining. I want to walk in her shadow, to be close.

No, not just close. One.

Hold and be held.

But I'm not worthy, even of her scorn.

But I long to see the derision in her eyes. That validates me. I want the lash of her tongue.

Tongue. Words. Touch.

Alive!

Help! What's happening? Let me in, let me talk. You're demeaning yourself, emptying yourself of life. Life? We're losing our self to a phantom.

November 19
Language for life

My dad was a salesman, always on the road. When he was at home, he was usually in the basement, fixing things. He didn't have much time for the girls in the family.

Mom worked, too, at the local hospital. She was a really shy person and wasn't any good at sticking up for herself. When Dad got mad, she crawled into her shell.

So I grew up without a language of exchange and love. I wasn't abused or beaten or bullied—just neglected and at a loss for words.

When puberty came, there was no discussion of bras or tampons or anything like that. It was as if we were just floating on the surface of life, without feelings or words.

My life went underground. I discovered sex , and that became my secret language—just for me.

I'm twenty-five and I've never slept with anyone.

I'm keeping my secret language just for me

We've started talking, you and I. It's been hard, not having words to express things or cope. But if we keep talking, we can find the words to move us out of the dark cave.

I like my women to be younger than me.

> *"My women." You sound like a sultan.*

All right. I like the women I date to be younger than me.

> *How long do you date them? Until they become older?*
> *Actually I've noticed lately that they keep on getting*
> *younger and younger.*

I'm a high-energy type. Most women can't keep up with me.

> *How could they? You drop them after a couple of*
> *months.*

They get boring. I need change.

> *And they, "your women"?*

They need change, too. Change is the law of life, you know.

> *I hate to say this to an old buddy, but you are talking*
> *and behaving like a smug, self-indulgent, priggish,*
> *egotistical adolescent. How old are you?*

Fifteen.

> *You're joking, of course, but there's a lot of truth in*
> *jokes. You're addicted to adolescence and adolescent*
> *sex. It's not a moral issue; it's a question of health and*
> *growing. How can you grow if your sex life is moving*
> *backwards?*

November 21
The bond of friendship

In my addiction, I've traveled a lonely path and neglected my friends. In my isolation, I stood off from their lives and their love.

Now that I'm on the road back to sanity, I'm picking up again the threads of friendship which are becoming stronger and stronger as the days go by.

I'm not afraid to talk to my friends about my needs, and, as I listen to them talk, I feel their pain and joy. Sharing brings us all together.

Coming back to my friends is like coming home.

It's as simple as that.

> *We've both been lonely and we've been hateful to each other. Let's talk about our new friendship, too.*

Yes. We can share that, too.

It's funny, but I feel kind of glad that I was scarred by my childhood.

>*Scarred or scared?*

Well, both really.

>*How come?*

It gives me a reason for writing. I write as compensation.

>*And the pain of your sex addiction?*

Yes. That's okay, too. I write to compensate for my affliction.

>*And the affliction?*

That's not so important, as long as I can write.

>*Are you scared that if you heal the wounds, you won't be able to write?*

Yes, that's it. Most of the writers I know are really messed up. But, you see, they have their writing. That's enough for us.

>*I know that's a trendy theory. But you won't lose the privilege of being yourself, just because you're cured. And if you are really yourself, you can still write . . . and talk, and live, and love. Why don't we give that a try?*

November 23
Ideal

Pornography's a kit. I cut and paste and create my ideal woman.

I decompose the pictures and make up the perfect figure. . . not too precise, of course. I hate sharp forms. The images I crave have a soft radiance, blurred and evocative.

I loathe nudity. There must be a shimmer, a haze of gauze and lingerie.

I half-close my eyes and see my mother there, in bits and pieces. Or a sister, or one of my grade-school teachers.

I'm a child again.

I disappear into the radiance of my beloved.

Why do you want an ideal that makes you disappear? Can't we find a place for real people, with real emotions? I think we need help.

It's impossible for me to concentrate when I'm lost in my sex addiction.

> *Why don't you give yourself permission to act out,
> then?*

Whose side are you on?

> *I can't bear to see you so restless and dissatisfied.*

Now you sound like Mom, wanting the best for her little boy. But I don't trust you. You're just giving me some rope so you can hang me.

> *All right. I was testing you. I'm glad you recognize
> Mom's voice. It's also the kind of thing you used to say
> to yourself.*

Yes, I remember. Mind you, it is hard to deal with this constant temptation. All I have to do is pick up the phone and she will be there.

> *Come on. Be a man. You can do it!*

Okay, Dad.

> *Too easy. These days you can pick up all the voices
> right away!*

Except my own.

> *Don't be hard on yourself. That used to be my role! We
> know it's difficult to break free of this addiction; but if
> we keep clear-headed and talk straight, we'll make it.*

Yes. And we'll even have some fun on the way!

November 25
Intimacy

I used to think that sex was a way of getting close: first the sex and then the closeness.

Now I know it's the other way around. Trust creates an environment where the risk of sex can be taken.

Intimacy depends on trust, and trust implies closeness and commitment. We can't know someone well unless we feel close to ourselves; then we can reach out and take the risk of a real relationship.

It feels good to be getting in touch again.

> *How scared you used to be! And how easy it was to criticize and condemn you!*

I know. I made myself so raw and vulnerable. And how you loved that!

> *Did I? Yes, I suppose I did.*

Well, that's quite an admission for an ex-dictator!

> *Thanks for the "ex"!*

Many groups are closed, rigid, self-satisfied. They are often based on fear or mutual admiration or self-righteousness.

At school, in the army, in business, I often joined such groups. I joined them for security, but I found only competition and intolerance.

When I joined a Twelve Step group, I expected to find the same sort of thing—a "holier than thou" attitude or even a kind of tyranny.

What I found was a place of openness, tolerance, and trust. People spoke from the heart and were not afraid to tell secrets that had remained closeted within them for years.

For the first time, I feel safe. In my group I can be myself at last.

I like you better when you feel safe. That helps me, too.

No more strife.

Well . . . I wouldn't go as far as that.

You will, one day, believe me.

November 27
Inheritance

Hey. I had a great talk with Mum today.

> *What did she say?*

You know, you were there, too.

> *Yes. But say it—you say it.*

She said she had all these voices inside: "You shouldn't have been walking there," "That was the wrong place to leave the car." "You know it's dangerous in the city." "You were asking for it, dressing like that."

> *And?*

She passed those messages on to me. She couldn't help it.

> *No, she couldn't, could she? And I took over where she left off, replaying those old tapes.*

What can we do now?

> *Change gears, change voices, change.*

Yes, let's.

> *I have to change, too, you know.*

Is that so hard?

> *No. Not really. Even moms can change.*

When Dad left, I was glad. I cried a lot in my room, but I said I never wanted him to come back. It was over.

"He seduced me, and I told Mom. She kicked him out. We're both glad." That's what I told my friends.

The boys came like flies around dead meat. They thought I was weird, but they knew I'd have sex with them anyway. And I did.

There was only one thing. They had to pay.

Oh, not just money. They had to say they cared about me, loved me, wouldn't leave me.

And they did. They said it and they left me.

Do you think I care?

> *Please listen. There's a place where we can talk about this—no, not with doctors or shrinks, but with other women who've been through the same kinds of things.*

They won't understand. I'm too weird.

> *We're all different, you know.*

I'm **too** different.

> *Won't you give it a try?*

Not today. No.

November 29
Obstacle race

You know, it's funny. I wanted Dad to be in the way, but he wasn't.

> *How do you mean, in the way?*

I wanted him to be there between me and Mother . . . not all the time, of course.

> *When?*

I don't remember exactly. When I was four or five, I think. It sounds crazy. . . .

> *Go on. I'm here.*

It's too crazy, really. I hate all this introspective family stuff.

> *It helps to talk.*

I wanted him to be where I thought he was, where he should be, in the middle . . . an obstacle, a shield. But it seemed (this is the really crazy part), it seems as if he, Dad, was kind of throwing me at Mom . . . you know, almost as if he wanted . . .

> *An out?*

Or an in! Anyway it was about then that he got out, for good.

> *And left you.*

Stranded.

> *It isn't the slightest bit crazy. And then that's when I took over . . . took over Dad's voice and started blaming you for his leaving. Now that was crazy! You've had a hard time, but we're talking now, and we can talk our way into new patterns that make sense!*

I used to make my position plain with my lovers: "I'm not
ready for a long-term relationship, I just want to enjoy what
we have together in the here and now."

"Here and now" really meant "Here today and gone
tomorrow"; when the sex began to pall or make real demands
on me, I'd be off and running.

One day I thought that I'd hate to die like this, running away
from yet another sex-only relationship.

Recovery started only when I felt that I could go on being an
addict forever and even die of my addiction.

Seeing death in these terms made me want to come back to
life.

> *That's good. You really weren't much fun to be with
> back then. You were "here today and gone tomorrow"
> for me, as well.*

Was I awful?

> *You were a selfish, cowardly, lecherous, treacherous
> prig.*

All that, and a prig, too? That's a bit much!

> *All right. Not a prig.*

335

December 1
Exchange

They say exchange is no robbery, but I feel robbed. Bereft.

    Isn't that because of the exchange you made?

Well, I gave her up, didn't I?

    Well . . .

Did I or did I not give her up?

    You did. For sex addiction.

Well that's what I said: I gave her up.

    But you feel robbed.

I gave her up and I feel robbed. That's what I said.

    She's still there. Your addiction is a tribute to Mom.

A tribute! How can you say that!

    She's still there, denied, profaned, but there. Every time. You think when you act out you deny her. But you confirm her, and affirm her power.

So I haven't exchanged a thing?

    You're on the way.

How far to go?

    Keep walking.

W̲e̲ talk about options, about choice, about sexual preference. But we addicts can only choose our way of going down into the abyss of loneliness and despair.

We know, deep down, that our lives are unmanageable and powerless and we are driven by our disease.

When I did hit bottom, there was a final choice: suicide or change.

I chose to get well, to get new power, to find a way back to sanity and peace of mind. I found love and support from those traveling the same path.

I like this path. It's the path of freedom of choice.

> *You should be proud. It really was a matter of life and death for both of us.*

And now we're both on the side of life.

> *Good choice!*

December 3
Second edition

I'll know when I meet the woman I'm destined to love; her image is already in my heart. Engraved.

I hear her voice, even. Not harsh, but rough in the throat, like the voice of a French actress. And her face . . . so familiar.

I've bought the scent that I'll give her on our honeymoon.

And the music—the same, of course.

I'll be a child again, innocent and trusting.

And she?

She'll betray me, like the other one.

They always betray you in the end.

I prefer whores.

> *You set yourself up for betrayal, don't you?*

She set me up, the first one.

> *And you keep **her** alive and the others dead. You cancel out their reality with your idealizing images.*

What can I do?

> *Let her image go and see **them** as they are. Then we can begin to live in the world of real people.*

338

When I was lost in the labyrinth of sex addiction, the world seemed grim and colorless and fearsome.

My compulsive behavior brought me no pleasure, and the days were long and empty, monotonous and full of melancholy like a winter's night.

The only laughter I heard was the cold, bitter laughter of scorn.

As I turn toward a new life, strengthened by the support of the group and the love of my friends, I am amazed to hear myself laughing again.

My body and my spirit had forgotten how good it feels to laugh out loud and let things go.

Now I love to laugh and savor the sheer delight in being alive.

> *Yes, how good it is to see you laugh and dance around.*
> *Your laughter puts us in touch again.*

May I have the pleasure?

> *The pleasure?*

The pleasure of this dance!

December 5
Doting

I never got to know a man before I fell in love with him. I longed for passion, and I idolized the image of the person who inspired me. I lived by proxy.

It never lasted—but that was okay because within a couple of days I'd find a replacement. I'd be hopelessly in love all over again.

And so it went on, and on and on. Each time, I found my idol, and then came the feet of clay. So I moved on.

In my group, when I told these stories, I expected admiration. After all, I was a free spirit, wasn't I?

The other people didn't say much, except to ask how I really felt and what I really wanted. I couldn't answer.

My life was empty. Sex was a narcotic that I desperately needed to fill the void.

I want to learn to love in a caring, adult way.

Doting is for dolts.

> *Well, that sounds a bit harsh! But I can see you're angry at yourself for being taken in by all those popular songs and images of eternal bliss.*

Eternal bliss! Give me affection and loyalty any time.

> *How about **now**?*

Now!

When I found out I had venereal disease, I knew I had to call the men I'd been sleeping with.

I sat down to make out the list and I came up with eleven names.

I was mortified. At the same time, deep down, I felt a kind of relief. **Now** I would have to give up sex.

All my life I've been addicted to sex with men. I used to take risks, going home with guys I hardly knew.

Going home, but never feeling at home. It was lonely and frightening most of the time.

But now all that is over. For good. I'll never, never have sex again.

> *You know, there's no need to be such an extremist—either eleven men at the same time, or a nunnery! When we really get into the Program, we'll get a balanced view on all this. Sex isn't All or Nothing, you know.*

December 7
Digging

I think the Program's going well, don't you?

> *For whom?*

The group. It's a really powerful group, isn't it?

> *It sure is. And you? How are you doing?*

I'm doing okay, don't you think?

> *What do you think?*

That's the question, isn't it?

> *What's the answer, then?*

I'm not really working my own program, am I?

> *Are you?*

No.

> *We'll have to keep on digging. The group's not a club, you know. It's a place to work.*

Work? I just want to **be**.

> *I know, but. . . .*

You're going to preach at me again.

> *No. You said it, when you talked about working the Program. Working the Program, that's what it's all about.*

I thought it was all about me.

> *You **and** the Program.*

You know, every time I used to feel anxious, zap! I acted out.
> *And now?*

Now I say: "Wait a minute. What's the trigger?"
> *Trigger?*

Yes. What's behind the anxiety, what triggered it?
> *Can you always find out?*

No. But it helps just to say to myself: "Just a moment—let's try and figure out what's going on here."
> *I see what you mean—a pause to break the spell.*

Yes. And then we can talk it over, you and I.
> *Sure. Talking is much more productive than acting out.*

It sure is.
> *Let's keep it up.*

Yes. Let's.
> *This sounds really healthy to me. And when we don't act out, we have all that surplus energy.*

Energy for work and play and love.
> *Love, not addiction.*

December 9
Being alone

I used to hate to be alone. I was afraid of being abandoned, as I was when I was a child.

In my recovery, I am gaining the confidence to spend time by myself, and I enjoy it. I realize that I don't always have to be in a sexual relationship or with other people.

Being happy alone is a sign of self-confidence and security. I can depend on myself. I trust myself. I don't always have to act out or run home to Mother.

Acting out is a strange kind of running away from myself. I'm glad I don't need to escape anymore.

> *I used to blame you for being weak and dependent. Then you were my little boy again. I don't need to do that anymore. We're growing up!*

Yes. And that's just fine with me!

I'm sitting here, tense and angry, going through withdrawal.

> *How do you feel?*

Terrible. I can't believe it's worth it.

> *It is in the long run.*

But I don't live in the long run. I live in the here and now.

> *But the here and now also exists in the long run; that's what we need to think about.*

I thought we were supposed to work the Program one day at a time.

> *Same thing. One day at a time eventually adds up to the long run. So you really can't lose, can you?*

I can lose my sanity, if I don't act out.

> *No. Acting out is insanity. You'll only feel betrayal and shame.*

You have all the answers today. And what's more you're being kind and helpful. I don't get it.

> *I'll tell you something. I laughed when you said we were going to join that group. But it's the best thing that's happened to both of us. I can see, feel, and touch the changes in us both.*

Yes. We're getting in touch, at last.

December 11
Partners

Sexual partners for me weren't partners at all, just objects. They were only there for me, for my pleasure. I made them partners in crime.

I didn't see them as real people, only as replicas, as pictures, as fantasies. If they made demands on me, I left them.

In my madness, I saw bodies as spare parts in the machine of my craving—interchangeable parts, just like the people I abused.

Recovery has helped me connect to people in a nonsexual way. I feel trust and loyalty. I don't want to run away. I give another man a hug and feel the embrace of a whole person.

Now the word "partner" has real meaning in my life.

> *Hi, partner! That all sounds familiar—our relationship was the same kind of thing. Always afraid of each other and always running away. It wore us both out.*

Yes, but not anymore.

> *Right. Maybe we'll get to be real partners . . . partners for life.*

Before I went into therapy, I couldn't remember anything that happened to me before the age of five.

My therapist asked me to write a sexual history. At first I refused but I finally agreed. I didn't have anything to write about before puberty. And yet every time I sat down to write, I felt there was something knocking at the inner door of my mind, trying to get in.

Finally, in my group another woman did her First Step and told us she had been sexually abused by an uncle when she was thirteen. He used to come and read to her in bed and fondle her; then one day, when her parents were out, he raped her.

I burst into tears and then felt faint. I went out and lay down in the women's room. One of the group came and sat and held my hand.

I cried a lot that day. And then, in the evening I went to see my therapist with a flood of memories . . . about my dead father whom I had loved.

My father who abused me.

And I protected his memory, acting as the censor. I'd even shame you if you started asking too many questions. I was your mother's voice, I guess, carrying on the same old deception.

December 13
Double standard

Remember last Thursday, when I said I was going to stop the car and pick up that prostitute, and you said "Sure, go ahead."

Did I?

You know you did. And then, when I decided not to, you said, "That's a good chance missed."

What of it?

Keep calm. Just listen to me for a change. Then, yesterday, you nudged me when we were passing the porno bookstore. Yes? I stopped like a good boy, went in and bought some hard stuff, and then went home and spread it all out on the bed. Do you remember?

Sure.

And then what did you do? You waited a minute or two, and then you started: "Swine, weakling, deviate, outcast, pervert." First the seductive carrot and then the sadistic stick. Funny, come to think of it, that reminds me . . .

Shut up!

. . . of Dad who kept all that stuff in the basement and then beat the hell out of me when he caught me with it. Yes! Of course! I'm onto your game now, partly because I've been talking to Karl about that group. Now I'm definitely going to join the group. And then we'll see, Smartypants.

Smartypants! You sound just like a child. You're raving! Just because you've picked up on a couple of minor contradictions. But I've got a lot more tricks up my sleeve. Just you wait and see!

The word *shame* means "covered," and often I've tried to disappear from the eyes of the world by hiding away in my shame.

As a child I turned against myself in contempt and hatred. I couldn't think of myself as a living person, only as an object of scorn. I ran from the gaze of others and covered myself in the black cloak of my shame.

Now each day I look at myself in the mirror and speak to myself with affection. I even like what I see and hear! I'm learning to confront myself without those old feelings of fear and humiliation.

Throwing away the cloak of shame is a vital step on the journey of recovery.

Yes, I can see you much more clearly now.

Does that make you feel more powerful, Big Boy?

No. More loving.

December 15
Another country

When I went back to visit my parents, it was always like going back to a home I always wanted but never had.

I'd think, This time it will be all right. I'll walk into the living room, and there'll be a fire in the hearth, and they'll both be there, welcoming. And I'll sit down. . . .

I sat down.

And Mom said, "How's that nice girl you talked about last time, Susie, wasn't it?"

Dad said: "Don't be stupid, Mary, he's told you that he doesn't like girls."

"Don't you call me stupid. He's my son, and I know. . . ."

"He's decided he wants to be a faggot, and that's an end to it."

Voices like rivers of fire, always running the same course and bringing the same pain.

Will they never change?

Will I?

> *You are changing. I hear it and feel it. Me, too. We are learning to listen to each other, you and I, and change the old records. And that's what matters. It seemed that those messages were engraved in stone, but it was only plastic!*

350

You sound angry again.

Again! Can't I just be angry?

You're almost always angry. That's why I said "angry again."

You sound priggish, if you want to know.

No. I'm feeling calm and strong, that's all. And I think that's why you're so angry.

What the hell do you mean?

You're angry because you can't jerk me around and make me squirm the way you used to. Ever since I've been in the group and learned to speak up for myself, you've been very quiet and very angry.

Wow, what a speech for a little boy!

Wrong again. I'm a thirty-year-old man, and glad to be me.

Are you really? Glad to be who you are and where you are right now?

Yes. You've said it, exactly.

Well, I must admit I'm impressed at the new tone in your voice. Six months ago you'd never have stood up to me like this. I wonder what it's going to be like to live as a mature adult. Can you help me learn, do you think?

December 17
Family romance

There was never much affection in my family as far as I could see, so I made some up.

My dad wasn't my dad. The reason he hated to touch me was because it reminded him that I was a bastard.

Mom was my queen. She wanted me as her lover because Dad was fat and ugly and always away on business. In my fantasy, she took me to her bed which was royal only for me. I merged into her and we became a magic alliance against the world. Us. Just us.

When I play on my own, I still act out my family romance. It's always the same. Always.

There will never be anyone else for me.

———————————

How could there be, darling?

That was great this evening in the group, when the guy did the Eighth Step about being willing to make amends.

Yes. I thought so, too. What struck you about it?

The fact that we need to learn to make amends to ourselves.

I agree. We've done each other a lot of harm, you and I. You with your shame-based little-boy talk....

And you with your sadistic angry-parent ranting and raving.

You asked for it.

My addiction wasn't my fault.

Same old excuses. I suppose it was Mom and Dad's fault!

Hey, wait a minute. Look where we are now, after only a few sentences! And I was saying how great it is to make amends....

To ourselves. Yes, I'm sorry.

I'm sorry, too. I'm really learning to like you. If only you'd...

Hold it right there! I know you were only kidding, but sometimes many a true word is spoken in jest. Let's be serious for a while and lie a little, shall we? No, let's just work at getting healthy!

December 19
Maps

When I look back I see my life as a map, with roads and tracks and pathways—a whole network of journeys.

Somewhere part of my life took the wrong turning and got blocked. Sex split off from affection. I was exiled from love.

Was it something I saw or did? Did someone else force me to take the wrong turning? Why did I take the single path of sex, divorced from love?

I need to reconnect with the missing path of caring and affection, to heal the split inside me.

That's what I need and find in the Program—a new network of relationships based on love and trust.

Yes, this is the map I've been looking for, and now I'm venturing into new and healing paths.

> *Yes, you were really lost, and I don't know why, either. But I took advantage of that to slander and abuse you. I helped you lose your way in the labyrinth of your addiction.*

Can we look for a new path together?

> *Yes. A path back to sanity and forward to love.*

Why can't you do anything right?

I'm trying.

> *Well, you're doing a lousy job as usual.*

Can't you leave me alone?

> *No. You can't be trusted.*

I'm beginning to trust myself.

> *That's new. What's happening?*

I'm feeling stronger now. I'm finding support and love in my group. It's a new family, and I feel welcomed.

> *That's good. Maybe you and I can get along better. I don't know though. . . .*

Yes, we can. As long as you get off my back and treat me like an adult, not a child. You know, I think we could really become friends.

> *Okay. Let's try, shall we?*

Yes. I'm feeling better already.

> *You look better. And you sound different.*

You, too. What's happening?

> *We're changing and growing together.*

December 21
Moments

When I was young, I always wanted the Great Love and the Big Moment. I wanted those rockets and stars and ecstasy I was always reading about.

I never found the Great Love, so I was left with the Big Moment.

I went out with a lot of guys who promised the the Big Bang, missiles, rockets, the stars . . . and left me in the pits.

I finally gave up on the Big Bang and went into drugs and booze.

Now I'm in recovery and I'm learning from my new friends in the group that there really isn't such a thing as the Big Moment.

Just lots of little moments to be sensed and grasped and cherished.

Yes, and part of the trouble was that I was always egging you on and leading you astray. Your recovery has helped me see things in a new way, too. Thanks for that, and thanks for all these little moments of joy.

I'm glad you're willing to do whatever it takes to recover from sex addiction.

Wait a minute. Who said "whatever it takes."

> *You want to recover, I know you do.*

Sure. But there are limits.

> *Like what?*

Well, there's Becky. I'm really fond of her, you know.

> *It's a one-hundred-and-fifty-percent supercharged sexual relationship, and you know it.*

Would you accept one hundred and twenty?

> *That's the cute and charming little sex addict talking. Trying to get off the hook. Why not be honest and steadfast. . . ?*

". . . for a change," you nearly said.

> *Please don't put words in my mouth.*

All right. I'm just testing you. Trying to make you mad, the way you used to be.

> *But we're both different now, aren't we? Come on, admit that you're sick and tired of this sex addiction stuff.*

Yes. I am. And I'll do whatever it takes to change.

December 23
Kings and pawns

My sex life used to be like a game: each day I worked on my strategy and planned new moves. I treated women like pawns in my royal game of sexual chess.

Of course I always thought I was winning, but in the end I always lost. I'd spend hours getting what I thought I wanted, but I never found what I really needed.

I had to hit bottom before I reached out for help. I was so blind that only real suffering and loneliness made me open my eyes and begin to see.

I joined a group, and for the first six months I just sat and listened. I heard my story being told over and over again by people whose lives, just like mine, had become unmanageable. I saw myself in these other people and finally decided to speak out and own my own addiction.

It's taken me a while to figure out that people are not objects and life is not simply a game.

> *I was there, all the time, and I played along with you in your childish games. Anything to keep you in my power!*

I'm glad we're out of those dumb games now.

My lover and I give ourselves treats when we're feeling down or when we need support.

We go to the local coffee house and have some fine Italian coffee. Or we eat something special. Or buy a book. Or go to a movie. Or buy each other some flowers. Or laze in bed. Or just do nothing. Just be.

I deserve treats; we all do. They needn't be grand or expensive; just special.

Treats make me feel special.

I am special. And now I believe it.

> *Yes, indeed. And I'm glad you realize it. I'm trying to help by treating you as a friend and not as a miserable little sinner!*

Let's go and have some of that Italian coffee!

December 25
Stress

Sex always makes me feel anxious, always.

Yes, I know. I can feel it.

What can I do about it?

Talk about it.

How?

Quietly and honestly.

Where?

In the group.

When?

Every week, and every day, if you like. All you have to do is pick up the phone and talk to someone in the group.

Yes. That's a relief! You know, when I was a kid, I never learned to talk about my sexuality—I don't even know the words to use or the feelings to talk about. But I'm not scared, the way I used to be. I can see how people in the group are learning to talk and to ask for help. It's like the family I always wanted but never had!

I feel the same way. And what's more, being in a new "family" is good for our relationship, too. No more shouting and arguing—doesn't it make a difference?

Yes. And you know what they say.

What?

They say it's love that makes the difference.

And you? What do you say?

I love you.

I thought sex was like an account you never had to settle.

Now I realize it's a credit card: buy now, pay later. And I've been paying for my sexual randomness—disease, loneliness, despair, disgust, terror.

I'm scared still, even though I'm in a group with people who understand and who care for me. They say they'll always be here for me, but can I trust them?

I guess the first thing is to trust myself. Now I'm not acting out, but starting to believe in myself.

I know it'll be a long, hard road, but if I take it one day at a time, I'll be healing all the way.

It's the journey that counts as well as the goal.

> *Right. And don't forget, we're in this together, old buddy.*

Can I trust you?

> *Take the risk.*

And you?

> *Shake hands on it.*

December 27
Home

They say "home is where the heart is." Do you believe that?

Oh, yes.

You sound so positive, so sure of yourself.

Now, why so offensive?

Me? Don't **you** get defensive. I just asked you a question.

Yes. And then attacked me for my answer. Nice guy!

It wasn't an attack; it was a defense.

But why? Whatever it was, why?

Because I'm scared I'll never go home.

Because of the addiction?

Yes.

But you're learning to love, now, beyond the addiction.

Yes, I believe that.

And in that beyond?

I don't know.

Think. No—feel!

Home?

Yes, home.

I still sometimes hear those old voices that all my life have been carping, jeering, slandering, keeping me down and out.

I hate them, and I hate myself, too, for not being strong enough to resist and come through.

From rage to sex is just one step. I pick up this sleazy guy in the park and bring him home and let him have his way and hurt me. I stand outside myself and watch. I relish the brutality. I think: "That's all I'm good for, abuse and pain."

He leaves. And then all the voices in my head go mad—fury, abuse, scorn, slander, hatred, disgust.

It serves me right. I'm down there in hell where I deserve to be.

Abuse, contempt, and rage, rage, rage.

> *I refuse to join in today. Listen, my dear, you're alive, vibrant, attractive. Let's work to move all that energy inside you to change your life and find new options. There's a group, just for people like us. Let's go. This is hell. We need to redirect all that power. We can do it, you'll see.*

I was losing my way again. It's so helpful and healing to hear you talk like that!

> *That's what it's all about—healing and becoming sane.*

December 29
Action

I can't do much today, I'm afraid. I'm regressing. Ugh!

> *What are you feeling?*

Anger. Shame. Fear.

> *Let's talk about it. . . . See, it's better when we talk.*

Yes, you're right. But when I'm down I always forget that.

> *We'll work on it together.*

Yes, let's. It feels so different when we talk. And you know what?

> *What?*

I think I love you . . . after all this time together. Yes, I really love you, after all these years.

> *That makes the difference. That makes my day.*

I'm feeling active and alive. It's love, isn't it, love that gives us energy?

> *Yes, it's love.*

Love is action, isn't it?

> *Yes. Oh yes.*

Sometimes I feel I've lost the ability to play—to become a child again, to live for the moment, to let myself go, to be inventive, curious, imaginative, alive.

What happened? My addiction cut me off from my precious child and turned me into a grim, obsessive robot.

I don't do what I really want to do; I simply obey my addiction. I work at having fun, but I never let go and enjoy myself.

What nonsense! What a ridiculous way to live! Enough! I want to change.

I **am** changing, moving forward. I'm changing, moving backward—toward the child I thought I'd lost but who is still alive and well within me.

> *You certainly were getting boring and nasty with your compulsions and obsessions. And how ridiculous some of them were!*

I know. I have to laugh at myself.

> *That helps us play.*

Yes. I'm glad we're going to play again.

December 31
Yes

There's one word I'd like us to say more often.
Yes?

> *That's it.*

It?

> *No. Yes.*

Well, which?

> *No, not which.*

What?

> *No, not which or what. You ask too many questions as
> it is. And you mumble.*

Okay. One more question. I'm speaking very slowly and
clearly now: what, or which, is this word you would like us to
say more often?

> *The word is yes.*

Just yes?

> *No. Not just yes, but yes to sanity, yes to recovery, yes
> to pain, yes to change, yes to love, yes to our self, yes
> to life. Yes.*

Yes. I see what you mean. Yes.

> *That's it. Now we've got it. Yes. And I love you. Now,
> this very moment. Yes.*

Contents by Title

371

July 15
That way

July 16
Euphoria

July 17
Missing

July 18
Shaming

July 19
Bodies

July 20
Love affair

July 21
Uncut

July 22
Powerlessness

July 23
Triumph

July 24
Icons

July 25
Bravado

July 26
Charming

July 27
Being happy

July 28
Nice guy

July 29
Sex in anger

July 30
Desertion

July 31
Accomplices

August 1
Hunt

August 2
Abandoned

August 3
Double bind

August 4
No problem

August 5
Blinders

August 6
Testing

August 7
Discord

August 8
Changing

August 9
Slippery

August 10
Power

August 11
Sex objects

375

December 30
  Playing

December 31
  Yes

Subject Index